I0646445

COMPLICATIONS

A NOVEL BY

STEPHEN TANNENBAUM

Red Engine Press
Pittsburgh, Pennsylvania

COPYRIGHT © 2019 BY STEPHEN TANNENBAUM

ALL RIGHTS RESERVED. NO PART OF THIS BOOK MAY BE REPRODUCED OR TRANSMITTED IN ANY FORM OR BY ANY MEANS, ELECTRONIC OR MECHANICAL, INCLUDING PHOTOCOPYING, RECORDING, OR BY AN INFORMATION STORAGE AND RETRIEVAL SYSTEM (EXCEPT BY A REVIEWER OR COMMENTATOR WHO MAY QUOTE BRIEF PASSAGES IN A PRINTED REVIEW OR DISTRIBUTED VIA THE INTERNET) WITHOUT PERMISSION FROM THE PUBLISHER.

COVER ART COPYRIGHT © 2019 ANA (KAT) GALLY

LIBRARY OF CONGRESS CONTROL NUMBER:2019953113
ISBN: 978-1-943267-72-9 TRADE PAPERBACK
ISBN: 978-1-943267-94-1- EBOOK

PRINTED IN THE UNITED STATES.

RED ENGINE PRESS
PITTSBURGH, PA

THE AUTHOR WISHES TO:

Dedicate this novel to his wife, Shirley, who was the first person to imagine him as a novelist and whose advice was invaluable to *Complications*;

Second, as all of his writing is dedicated, to his mentor of many years, now deceased, Monty Culver, Professor Emeritus of English Writing, University of Pittsburgh;

And wishes to thank for their tireless efforts on behalf of the work his first readers, Riv Swartz and David Harry Tannenbaum (novelist, longtime friend and fraternity brother, no relation).

COMPLICATIONS

A NOVEL

CHAPTER 1

Tom Murdoch's favorite Beatles' tune played over and over in his head as he and Bobbi, his three-year-old beagle, strolled the neighborhood on their daily afternoon walk. He couldn't help humming *Norwegian Wood*. Once a tune bubbled to the surface of his brain, it would hang around to haunt him for hours. November breezes danced around, scattering the crisp, russet leaves over sidewalks and lawns. Bobbi got a kick out of the crunching and crackling noises they made as she waded through heaps of them.

The air was fuggy with Fall.

They were a handsome pair, man and dog. Bobbi was wearing a red vinyl jacket that strapped around her belly and across her chest. She looked very spiffy. Tom had curly black hair and bright green eyes he inherited from his mother, and he had his father's broad shoulders and Irish good looks. He was wearing jeans, a thick winter vest over a heavy long-sleeved shirt, and a knitted cap pulled over his ears against the chill.

Sunny Fall afternoons in Pittsburgh— he and Bobbi loved them.

Suddenly a man darted out from between parked cars to confront them. He was built as wide and squat as a tank. A dark-skinned black man with a fierce expression on his face, wearing a black quilted jacket and a ball cap on a large head that looked as if it were sprouting dreadlocks. The knife that he waved in front of Tom's face had an illegal eight inch blade.

His voice was raspy, as if he had a bad cold, and he sounded as angry as he looked. He said, "Gimme your wallet, ofay muthafucka."

Tom didn't like the look of that knife or the way he was being threatened with it. Fear? He must have felt fear, but surprisingly little. He seemed to have slipped into a never-before experienced, trance-like state that had become part of him, without his realizing it, from years of self-defense classes.

He said to the knife-wielding man in a robotic tone of voice he didn't recognize as his own, "What are you going to do if I don't hand over the wallet?"

"I'm gonna cut you up in little pieces and feed you to that fuckin' mutt."

Bobbi was no mutt, she was pure beagle through and through, and she took offense at being called a mutt. Her growl was not very menacing, but she tried.

"Oh, okay," Tom said. He moved as if to retrieve his wallet. Instead he drew the Heckler & Koch .45 caliber pistol that he carried, on duty and off, in the hollow of his back in a holster clipped to his belt. He pointed it where he guessed his assailant's belly button was and noisily jacked the slide. He said, "Now what?"

The black man blinked and swallowed.

"I'm gonna bug out as fast as my ass will carry me."

He turned as if he intended to go but immediately turned back, and for no reason that made any sense to anyone who heard about the incident later, he lunged to stab Tom.

Without thinking about it—and a good thing, for there wasn't time to think about it—Tom pulled the trigger twice and put two holes in the center of the man's chest, the impact knocking him off his feet and onto his back. The noise echoed off the facades of houses up and down the tree-lined street, amazingly loud. Tom's ears rang. Again without a thought, or without a thought he would recall later, he strode over to the prone figure, careful not to step on the outstretched arms, and checked the neck for a pulse. None. Lying there, the body looked like a bundle that had tumbled out of an auto mechanic's ragbag. The knife had fallen out of his hand and came to rest in the gutter, a few feet away. Tom refrained from the impulse to touch it.

Bobbi tugged at the leash, which startled Tom, who seemed to come awake out of a dream. He gave Bobbi some slack. She circled frantically, tipped up and did her business, which he immediately bagged.

* * *

That story, in almost those exact words, was the story Tom later told the detectives of Division 4. It was the truth, as far as it went. Only it was not the whole truth.

Chapter 2

Tom had all the Pittsburgh Police divisions on speed dial in his cell phone, although he had ended his employment on the City force three years ago, when his brother, Arthur, was elected City & Allegheny County District Attorney. Tom worked out of Arthur's office now as a County detective. He searched his pockets for that cell phone, only to discover that he'd left it in his apartment. Damn! Division 4 was no more than three blocks away, close enough that Tom guessed they might have heard the shots. The body was blocking the sidewalk, but there were no pedestrians in sight to trip over it. Bobbi led the way toward Division 4, his master in tow.

As they walked Bobbi kept stopping to look back to see if Tom was all right, worried that he wasn't.

That he had shot and killed a man kept coming back at Tom like an echo from a dream.

He wondered who would have jurisdiction in the shooting: the city, being the site of the incident; or Allegheny County, being his employer, the legal owner of the weapon and the issuer of his concealed carry license. He wasn't sure. What he was sure of was that his brother was going to be pissed. Arthur had already mounted his re-election campaign, and Tom knew Arthur was counting on the backing of the black community to help him win a second term as D.A.

He had shot and killed a man.

Tom thought, for the umteenth time in his life, If I could only take that back…

He wondered if a shit storm was coming.

* * *

Arthur P. Murdoch—Artie—was not just Tom's brother, he was his big brother. A different thing altogether, as those who have a big brother are aware. From the day Tom was born, almost ten years and two miscarriages after Arthur—it was no secret that Tommy was the beloved accident—Arthur became his advisor and protector. He was there to clear the way for Tommy if he could; if not, he was prepared to fight Tommy's battles for him. Tommy was never certain whether Artie wanted to or if he felt he had no choice, that his little brother was his responsibility. It was a clichéd situation.

Tommy understood that he too was a cliché, the epitome of a little brother: unpredictable, easily distracted, scattered, a magnet for trouble; always stepping in it. Artie may not have been aware of it, but whenever he saw Tommy coming, he got a certain look on his face. Even before he would say, 'Welcome, bro,' or 'Hey, Tommy, how they hanging,' and 'Oh, shit, what is it this time' look would turn down the corners of his mouth and drop his eyelids like sagging blinds. Not a look Tommy was happy to see, not a look he was proud to earn.

* * *

Bobbi led the entire way to the Division 4 Precinct House, with Tommy merely hanging onto her leash. When he was able to focus, he discovered they were standing on the sidewalk in front of Division 4.

The House, as those assigned there called it, was located near the intersection of Northumberland Street and Shady Avenue in the Squirrel Hill neighborhood; it had a split personality, being the headquarters of both the police and fire departments of the city's Fourth Division. It was a Depression Era construction of soot-stained granite blocks, a sight that Tom had always found to be depressing on the outside, and its narrow, low-ceilinged corridors painted an institutional shade of green made it equally depressing on the inside.

Since Medical Examiner Sam Goldenson's HQ was a long way off in downtown Pittsburgh, Tom thought he might save time and possibly spare the neighbors the fright of stumbling over the body he had left back on the sidewalk. Maybe he could convince the EMTs to retrieve the body. He led Bobbi into the ambulance bay, where they found two EMTs washing their vehicle.

The taller of the two men was wiping the rear windows with paper towels. With hardly a glance in Tom's direction, he called out, "Hey, no pets allowed in here."

Tom assumed the other EMT was the ranking member of the team, since he was doing none of the work. He was as big and wide as a one-seat Port-a-Potty. His name tag said, BAILEY. His head was shaved and polished, and he had a weightlifter's shoulders. Tom would have to handle Bailey carefully, because city cops didn't think much of county cops, and Tom worried that maybe the animosity extended from city EMTs to county detectives.

Tom informed Bailey that there was a dead body three blocks down on Plainfield Avenue, shot twice in the chest and bleeding on the sidewalk.

"Yeah?" He looked skeptically at Tom and Bobbi. "Who shot him, you?"

"I did, yes," Tom said, and identified himself as Tom Murdoch, County Detective.

"County, eh?" With a smirk on his face and an impish glint in tiny eyes that were too close together, the big EMT nodded his shiny head in Bobbi's direction and said, "That there yer partner?"

Bailey's partner, the younger one with the paper towels, turned his attention from the ambulance's windows and brayed like a jackass in appreciation of his boss's sense of humor. His name tag read WOLOWITZ.

Bailey began quoting proper procedure to Tom, as if Tom didn't know the proper procedure: that the shooting was to be reported to the city detective squad. His emphasis was on city and he indicated toward the ceiling with a thumb, which Tommy took to mean, upstairs. The detectives would start an investigation, he said, they would notify the M.E. and the Crime Scene Investigators.

Bailey said, "Dead bodies ain't the job of EMTs."

Tom got a little bit pissed at Bailey's tone, and that surprised him. He usually had better control of his temper—usually—but what had transpired three blocks down the street hadn't been the usual. He had killed a man. He tried a few deep breaths, with little effect.

He said, "I just thought you'd want to spare one of the local citizens the shock of stumbling over a dead body on the sidewalk. But I get it, you just washed the vehicle. You don't wanna get it dirty."

Wolowitz, jackass that he was, had the presence of mind to move into position between his boss and Tom. Bobbi growled, her fur was up. EMT Wolowitz told all three of them, the two men and the dog, to back off and cool down. He pointed Tom in the direction of the detective squad, which was housed upstairs on the second floor. His boss, Bailey, looked as if he wanted to tell them another place to go.

* * *

Bobbi, being a short-legged beagle, always dealt with stairs cautionly, so she and Tom carefully climbed one set of stairs. On the landing before the second set, they came face to face with a uniformed female police officer. Tom thought it was splendid the way she filled out her navy blue trousers and light blue blouse. Her name tag read, CALLAHAN.

She said, "What can I do you for, handsome?"

Without thinking Tom replied, "Well, for starters, you can frisk me." What was he saying? He had always been shy with all women except his mother. But he went on, "Take your time, make it a thorough search." He couldn't believe that those words had come out of his mouth; nor could Bobbi, who turned a wary eye in his direction. Maybe he was still operating on reflexes, like a robot. He felt dizzy and off balance.

Callahan, standing in front of him with her arms akimbo, looked broad and formidable, as husky as Tom was himself, but he attributed that to the effect of her being dressed in regulation uniform blues and full weapons belt. She was as tall as Tommy, too, though the patrolman's brogues she was wearing may have added an inch. She had skin the color of malted milk and hair as slick and black as patent leather, except for a patch of hair that was dyed pink above her forehead. Her hair was cut in a layered style and shaved close at the ears. And she had eyes. Eager hazel eyes bright with intelligence.

She said with a grin, "I wasn't talking to you,

Ugly, I was talking to the little guy."

"Little girl," he said. "Bobbi, with an i."

"Well, Bobbi with an i, put 'er there." She leaned over and offered her hand, not knuckles up as most people do to a dog, but palm up, and Tom was damned if Bobbi didn't shake paws with her.

He found his tongue and told Officer Callahan in brief what had happened three blocks down on Plainfield, showed her his photo I.D. He also tried to hand over his County Detective's credentials and his H&K.

"Hold on to those, sweetie," she said. "You can give them to the detectives upstairs. Meanwhile, you calm down, okay? I think you're still in shock."

What did she mean by that? Tom felt....

He looked at his hands—she was right, he had the yips.

Callahan led the way up to the detective squad room. Maybe she was right, Tom thought, maybe he was in shock, but not so much that he didn't enjoy watching her butt as she led the way.

* * *

The second floor of Division 4 was as depressing as the first floor, only even more in need of renovation. It was deathly quiet except for the occasional alarming ring of a telephone. Tom couldn't imagine his workplace, the downtown city-county building, being so quiet even at midnight on a weekend. The walls were the same depressing shade of green as the ones downstairs, only when he glanced up at the ceiling he saw flaking paint, like a bad case of dandruff.

Two detectives were on duty—Michaels and Goldberg, the one a young African-American and the other a white guy who looked old enough to have been there on duty since the Great Depression. Tommy approached the older man's desk, badge in hand where it could be clearly seen, and said, "Detective Goldberg, I'm County Detective Thomas..."

"I'm Goldberg," said the young detective, sitting at an adjacent desk. "What, a black man can't be Goldberg? You never heard of Whoopie Goldberg? Sammy Davis Jr.? Why couldn't I be the Jew?"

Callahan stepped in. "Aw, come on, fellas, cut the crap. Give the guy a break, he's been through a lot. Okay?"

The two detectives nodded their apologies, saying they were sorry, they had to do something to break up the monotony. He must know what it was like, things had been quiet lately. There was not much crime in Division 4.

Tom said, "You can't mean the Tree of Life Synagogue shooting was not much crime."

Goldberg said, "No, we don't mean that. The synagogue shooting was much crime, too much crime, but that was then and this is now, and things are back to boring normal again."

Michaels nodded agreement, said he hoped Thomas had come with something interesting. Said they were only an hour into their shift and were already bored stiff.

They were only an hour into their shift? Tom didn't say anything, but he couldn't imagine what they'd look like at the end of it. Goldberg looked rumpled and worn out, as did the suit he was wearing, obviously a *Goodwill Industries* special. Goldberg had a rosy blush of a complexion, which reminded Tom of his 2008 Dodge Dart—it and Goldberg both showed a lot of rust.

Tommy was unsure of Detective Michaels' age, maybe he was forty. Twenty years younger than Goldberg, for sure. Michaels was wearing a green cord sport jacket and a tartan tie loosely knotted and flung carelessly over his shoulder. He looked bored but smart. When he heard Tom's last name was Murdoch, he blinked. But he didn't say anything.

Tom began the narrative of what had occurred three blocks down on Plainfield: that he and Bobbi were taking their usual afternoon walk on their usual route, when all of a sudden..."

As Tom was talking, Bobbi sidled over to Callahan and began rubbing suggestively against Callahan's trouser leg. She said, "Excuse me, Mr. Murdoch. Your dog..."

Tom was unhappy to hear that he was now Mr. Murdoch, no longer Sweetie. He really wanted her to call him Sweetie. *Oh well*, he thought, *Murdoch is my name*. At least he wasn't Ugly any more. He tugged on Bobbi's leash; the beagle looked disappointed, but reluctantly left Callahan's side.

Tom continued the narrative: that all of a sudden they were accosted by a man with a long-bladed knife…that he threatened to kill Tom and Bobbi too, if he didn't hand over his wallet…that Tom had drawn his H&K instead of the wallet and held it where the man could plainly see it. That at first the man seemed prepared to skedaddle, but inexplicably changed his mind and lunged at Tom, forcing him to discharge his weapon. End of narrative. The truth. As far as it went. Oh, and did he mention the guy was a black man?

Michaels took possession of Tom's badge and weapon, and stowed them in a drawer of his desk. Made out a receipt and handed it to Tom. He was curious to know if Tom had ever discharged his weapon before, other than at a firing range. No, he hadn't. And how did Tom feel, having shot somebody? Lousy. Michaels said that he had asked because he, Michaels, had never shot anything but a paper target.

Michaels had heard that it changed you, somehow. Tommy wasn't sure, it was too soon to tell.

After Goldberg phoned the Medical Examiner's office, they sat Tom down with last month's issue of *People* Magazine and told him to stay put while Michaels and Goldberg headed off to the scene. Callahan got some water for Bobbi and coffee for Tom.

He could hardly hold onto the paper cup—he still had the yips.

CHAPTER 3

Tom found it hard to follow Detective Michaels's orders to stay put in the Division 4 squad room. He tried but failed to focus his attention on the revealing photos of big-breasted starlets in *People* Magazine. He managed to force down a second cup of the sludge Officer Callahan apologized for calling coffee. He paced the worn hardwood floors and climbed the walls, his mind churning over and over the fact that only an hour or two before, he had killed a man.

He knew very well what was happening three blocks down from the stationhouse: uniformed officers had cordoned off the area with crime scene tape; the detectives were searching for and then marking the locations of spent shell casings; they were bagging any evidence they were able to find, including the perp's illegally long-bladed knife; they were knocking on doors in the neighborhood looking for eyewitnesses. In short, they were processing the crime scene. God knew, Tom had helped do it more than a few times himself years ago when he wore the blue uniform. At first he imagined the officers holding back the curious neighbors and the reporters and TV camera crews who were hoping to get some footage for the 6 o'clock news. Then he imagined the headline on page one of the newspaper—D.A.'s brother kills Black Man. He imagined the words 'black man' just that way, big and bold. A few more deep breaths. This was a quiet neighborhood, true enough, but for how long? He felt he was about to leap out of his skin.

Officer Callahan's shift ended at 6 o'clock. Before she left she told him she had been in touch with the D.A.'s office to fill them in on what had happened.

Tom asked, "Was he angry? My brother, Artie? Was he angry?"

She didn't know, she hadn't spoken to him. She spoke to a woman named Tangretti. Of course she did. As Tom well knew, everybody who called the D.A.'s Office in hopes of speaking to the D.A. had to speak first to Marge Tangretti. Then, if it were okay with Marge Tangretti, which it frequently was not—even if you happened to be the D.A.'s brother—but if it were okay with Marge Tangretti, then and only then could you speak to Artie.

Callahan said, "Are you listening to me, Sweetie, or am I talking to the wall? Ms. Tangretti said for you not to bother going downtown tonight. By the time you'd get there, they'd be gone. Go home, get a good night's sleep. Good advice, that, I'd say," she added. "Leave everything to us cops. You can talk to your brother in the morning." She nodded to him, shook paws with Bobbi and departed.

Any kind of a night's sleep, good or bad, seemed to Tommy to be good advice, especially since it came from both Marge and Officer Callahan. But the very idea of sleeping, even just closing his eyes, filled him with dread of nightmares.

* * *

It took a total of four hours for the detectives of Division 4 to cut Tom and Bobbi loose. He was weary of pacing the squad room floor or sitting on his ass doing nothing and then answering the same questions over and over again. He led Bobbi home, fed her and tucked her into her crate. He thought about a pizza. He thought about takeout Chinese. What a day! He fell onto his bed fully clothed and dropped unconscious into a restless night of fending off attackers with machete-length knives and grappling to overcome the black-winged Angel of Death; and between those nightmares were dreams of Officer Callahan.

CHAPTER 4

Tom didn't know how predictable the weather was in other towns. He hardly had the opportunity to visit other towns except on law enforcement training assignments, and in those circumstances he found himself too busy to notice the weather very much. But he knew what it was like in Pittsburgh, and in Pittsburgh a person was rarely able to tell by a look at the morning sky what sort of day it was going to be. Never in the Fall or Winter; seldom in the Spring or even in Summer. Tom found that the weather in the 'burgh was as unpredictable as its people.

Take any rough morning for instance: Tom would wake up all twisted in the bed clothes, his PJs damp with sweat, groggy, eyes sticky with sleep, feeling grumpy and out of sorts. A look out the window would reveal dark, scudding clouds and pedestrians holding umbrellas and leaning against the wind. But if he managed to drag his miserable self to the closest IHOP and sit down to buttermilk pancakes with maple syrup and maybe blueberries, with bacon on the side and two mugs of strong sweetened coffee, by the time he had managed to deal with all of that, miraculously, he might discover that the sun had come out.

So it happened that morning when Tommy stepped onto the sidewalk of Baum Boulevard from the IHOP, with a tall stack of pancakes, berries, bacon and joe under his belt. The prospects for the day, if not bright, at least felt as if he were not walking beneath a little black cloud. On that sort of upbeat half note, he climbed into his Dodge Dart and headed downtown.

* * *

Due to the high cost of parking in the City parking garages, most people who worked Downtown wisely chose to park their vehicles on the streets of nearby neighborhoods close to a transit stop—Pittsburghers hated to walk—and they would ride a bus to work. Not Tommy. One of the perks of his job (and it would be wrong to think that being the D.A.'s brother hadn't figured into it) was access to one of the half dozen parking spaces allotted to the D.A.'s Office in the lot beneath the City-County Building. A free space all to himself. He surrendered that spot to one of his brother's assistant D.A.s, which earned him the gratitude of that Assistant D.A. and a sisterly peck on the cheek from her that Tommy very much enjoyed. But that was not why he surrendered that parking spot. He chose instead to accept a spot in the underground lot beneath the Public Safety Building, which is two long blocks east of the City-County Building. Tommy loved walking from one building to the other, no matter what the weather, among the bustling swarm of pedestrian traffic, accompanied by the honking, tooting, chuffing din of Grant Street vehicular traffic. The comings and goings of Pittsburgh's rush hour. He would not want to miss them for the world, but that too was not why he chose to surrender his spot.

Tommy applied his special brand of logic to the situation: were he to park each working day in the basement of the City-County Building, he would logically take the elevator from the basement to his little cubbyhole of an excuse for an office on the third floor or, again, take the elevator directly to his brother's suite of offices on four. That would never find him entering the building by the front entrance, and he wanted to use the front entrance.

On the building's front stoop, as if to casually greet every single person who was about to enter the building, there was a remarkable likeness in bronze of Richard Caliguiri, a former mayor of Pittsburgh. A beloved former mayor of Pittsburgh who died when Tommy was still in high school. Caliguiri was beloved for a number of practical political reasons, but mostly he was beloved because he was a really friendly guy of good intentions, good humor and good character. Tommy never knew him, never even met him, but Artie had known him and Artie had loved him. If Tommy were of a vindictive mind, he might have thought Caliguiri was the kind of brother Artie really wanted instead of the kind of brother he'd been saddled with. But Tommy was not of a vindictive mind.

Anyway, he liked to approach the building each morning by the front way, stopping to wish the statue of Mayor Caliguiri a good morning. Sometimes, if no one were lingering nearby to overhear him talking to a statue and think him a nutcase, Tommy would tell the statue his troubles or share his hopes for the day. It would not be a mistake to consider the statue of Mayor Caliguiri, or at least the virtues the statue represented, to be Tommy's moral compass. It certainly served a function in his life that no other human being served except his mother, may she rest in peace.

* * *

He was anxious to discuss yesterday's events with His Honor the Mayor, but when he had covered the blocks of Grant Street and reached the front of the City-County Building, he found the statue surrounded by a noisy crowd of elementary school students, their teacher and two chaperones. The Mayor had no time for Tommy that morning. Oh well, Tommy thought, His Honor wasn't going anywhere, and Tommy wasn't going far. There would be time later. He walked around the crowd of students and entered the lobby.

* * *

The City-County Building was erected in 1917 and the vast amount of granite used in the outer construction made it typical of public buildings of its time. The lobby of the building, two-football fields in length, reflected the wealth of the era with the use of Italian marble and gilded wood trimmings to line the doorways of upscale jewelry and clothing shops, while the upper stories reflected more of the austerity of the Depression, as did the schools, libraries, post offices and police stations in all the neighborhoods of Pittsburgh, with dark mahogany woodwork, heavy oak doors with panels of wire-re-inforced glass, green-painted plaster walls, heavy oak banisters. And a redolent pall hanging over everything, an odorous concoction of floor polish, disinfectant and cigar smoke.

But necessity brought change to the City-County Building, necessity first when it was discovered that asbestos had been used to insulate all the pipes which, of course, were located in very inaccessible places. Necessity again in the form of previously undiscovered roofing leaks that had allowed mould, both black and green, to tenant other inaccessible places. At great expense to the taxpayers of the City and County, and great inconvenience to occupants of the various office suites, the building was brought up to a standard more resembling that of the present day. But the marble floors were still hard on the feet, the elevators still staggered upward and lurched to a halt at each level, the women workers constantly complained of being—mysteriously—too hot and too cold at the same time. Of course one could always open a window—not! They were all painted shut. And although it had been a smoke-free workplace for almost a decade, the smell of cigar smoke still lingered.

In other words, like everyone else who worked in the City-County Building, Tommy had a special place in his heart for it. It was his second home. For his daily aerobic workout, he took the stairs to his cubbyhole on the third floor.

For Tommy the word home conjured up feelings of warmth and comfort:

> *He visualizes the living room of the old Murdoch family duplex on Chislett Street. Outside, it is a blustery winter evening, inside they are snug and warm. There is a fragrant, crackling fire in the fireplace. Artie is trying to coax the car keys from Dad. Tommy is curled up on the floor near the fire dressed in his PJs; Mom has brought him a glass of warm milk and a toasted cheese...sigh.*

The third floor of the City-County Building was a vast open space subdivided into cubbyholes for paralegals and Allegheny County detectives like him. It tended to convey a feeling of being no more than a lowly egg of a dozen lowly eggs in a large foam carton. But that morning, no sooner had Tommy dropped his butt into the swivel chair behind his little desk in his own little cubbyhole than those feelings of inferiority ebbed away. A small sign at what served as an entrance to his cubbyhole stated authoritatively that he was Thomas P. Murdoch, County Detective. He wasn't a bad person, was he? He had shot and killed a man. But an instinctive act of self-preservation was justified, wasn't it? Well, at least he was at home.

Rap! Rap!

His reverie was interrupted by a knocking on the wooden partition of his cubbyhole. It was Marge Tangretti. She always knocked even though there was no door.

Marge Tangretti had been Arthur's assistant forever, or so it seemed. Tommy remembered his dad saying that Marge was Artie's gal Friday and Tommy always wondered, Why just Friday and not the other days of the week? He didn't get it. Marge started out as a legal secretary with the firm of Ferguson, Finneran & Boyle. When those august partners hired Arthur fresh out of law school, Marge was assigned to help the young Mr. Murdoch to get his legal feet wet. Later when Artie decided to make the leap into private practice, Marge leapt right along with him. Tommy was a rookie on the City Police Force at the time. When Artie was offered a job by then Allegheny County D.A. Tino Petropolis, he accepted with the proviso that Marge Tangretti be hired too. With Marge as his right hand and with Tommy jumping from the City Police to the County force, Arthur Murdoch served as an assistant D.A. until Mr. Petropolis's retirement. Only then did he run for D.A. on the Democratic ticket. And he won! And Tommy moved from the uniformed County Police to plainclothes County Detective.

So there was a lot of history connecting Arthur and Marge and Tommy. The way she treated Tommy, you'd swear she was his big sister. As Artie had, so she seemed to have willingly taken Tommy on as her responsibility. He wished she hadn't. It was not a role he cherished, being her burden, her little brother.

Marge stood in his door-less doorway, arms akimbo, head wagging. She said, "Tommy, Tommy, Tommy…."

* * *

Marge was a tall woman, almost as tall as Tommy, and unlike his little love handles, there was not an ounce of fat on her sleek, five-foot-eight inch frame. There was just enough of Marge and in just the right places, not what you would expect of an Italian-American woman on the wrong side of forty.

Once Tommy asked her how she managed to keep her slim figure. She didn't take offense at his having looked her over—he breathed a sigh of relief.

She replied, "Simple. I lay off the pasta."

That was Marge. Years ago when he first met her, Marge reminded him of a co-ed he had a huge crush on when he was working toward an associate degree in Law Enforcement at CCAC. Tommy could still picture that coed, though it was years ago. She was just like Marge: tall, well built, shoulder length dishwater blonde hair and an angular face with an overbite that drove him nuts. Tommy was sure she loved him, too, but…no. Her name was Joanne … something. That's all, just Joanne. It was too long ago.

Marge claimed she was married. She wore a wedding ring to prove it, but she never brought her husband to the City-County Building or to any of the annual Christmas office parties. Tommy questioned her husband's existence. He couldn't imagine how Marge could have found the time to acquire a husband or to maintain a relationship with one. She was too busy managing the D.A.'s Office, keeping Artie's calendar, liaising with officials of the County's various departments, fundraising for Artie's re-election campaign, collecting his suits from the dry cleaners and occasionally babysitting Tommy's nieces, Artie's children. In short, keeping all those wheels turning and greased, and to Tommy's sorrow, minding him, Artie's little brother.

* * *

Marge gave Tommy one of those sisterly hugs women were fond of giving where they lean into a person and clasp the top half of their body to the top half of the other person's body. In Tommy's case, he didn't mind Marge leaning the top half of her body against him, even though he hadn't yet removed his hat and coat.

She said, "Tommy...."

He said, "Marge, I swear. All I was doing was the usual, walking Bobbi."

"She wasn't hurt, was she? The report didn't say anything about Bobbi."

"I killed a guy, Marge."

"You're telling me, you did. You killed a black guy, Tommy. You really stepped in it this time."

"I was less than four blocks from my apartment, in my own neighborhood, minding my own business. Walking my dog, like I do every day."

"Yeah yeah, I know. I saw a report last night on the 11 o'clock news. They showed an empty area of sidewalk cordoned off with crime scene tape. By empty I mean empty, the M.E. had already hauled off the body. All they had to show viewers was an empty patch of sidewalk with little markers where they found the shell casings, and a police vehicle with its roof bar flashing. Oh, and the on-camera talent admitting she had no idea what or who happened there. Stay tuned.

"So, not much to see, thank God. But still, Tommy, you stepped in it, all right. Come on, he's waiting for you." Marge said he as if she were referring to St. Peter and it happened to be Judgment Day.

Marge led the way, setting a pace Tommy had trouble keeping up with. The clack of her heels echoed down the crowded corridor. Ordinarily he wouldn't have minded bringing up the rear as Marge led the way toward the bank of elevators, busy as the hall-ways usually were on workday mornings. To watch her, an expert interact-er with people, as she greeted everyone she passed, conducting business as she went, offering to do favors, thanking those who had done favors for her, for the D.A.'s personnel or for her boss, the D.A. himself. To watch as she proceeded was an education unto itself. To say nothing of the pleasure of watching her shapely behind as she hustled along the way. But that morning he wished there were reins to tug on to slow her pace—he felt she was leading him, not to his brother but to the guillotine.

CHAPTER 5

They rode up to the fourth floor in a crowded, oppressively silent elevator, and as they made their way through the D.A.'s reception area, past Marge's private office, and by a private entrance into Artie's sanctum, Tommy's ears rang with an imaginary jailer's warning call, Dead Man Walking. But he was wrong. There was Artie on his feet and hurrying toward him, not with that 'What is it this time?' look on his face but with concern written all over it. When he saw that Tommy was still in one piece, concern was replaced by relief.

The Murdoch brothers were a mixed ethnic bag. Their dad was a New York-born Irishman, with a politician's exuberant personality, the agile strength of a fireman—which was what he was, first in New York City then later in Pittsburgh—and devilish good looks. Their mom used to say her husband was an Errol Flynn look-alike. Flynn was long before Tommy's time, but he watched a lot of old movies on late night TV.

Their Mom's people, on the other hand, were originally from the Ukraine. Tommy was told people from the Ukraine were really tough customers; he could testify that his Mom certainly was, but she was also very smart and a beauty to boot. She had curly black hair worn long to her shoulders, and big beautiful intelligent green eyes. Tommy saw her whenever he looked in the mirror.

Artie's resemblance to Flynn, his lean, agile body, his personality, his political ambitions, he inherited all those from their Dad. Their Mom was overheard describing Artie to one of her next door neighbors:

"My Arthur is a glad-handing devil of a Mick with a Yiddisher kop.

* * *

So the Murdoch brothers were half Irish Catholic and half Ukrainian Jewish. Arthur had inherited all the good stuff, the looks, the personality and the smarts. At least Tommy thought so. Artie had excelled in school, charmed the ladies, managed to earn the trust and respect of the men, and got votes from them both. They said of Tommy, although it was true that he had inherited much of his mother's eastern European good looks, they said of him that he had inherited his big brother and didn't need anything else.

* * *

Artie extended his hand to shake with Tommy, but when Tommy reached for it Artie poked his fist toward Tommy's crotch to make him juke. And when he did juke, Artie smacked Tommy upside the left ear. Brothers!

Artie said, "See those reflexes, Marge? Dead slow, right? But normal for him. I told you he'd be okay."

Marge said, "I think you should cut your brother some slack, Sir." She frowned at the little-boy antic display she had just seen from her boss. "He's had a traumatic experience."

"You're right, consider me chastised. Here, Tommy, have a seat."

Artie led his brother to the chair across the desk from his own. Once they were both seated and Marge was in her accustomed position one step behind and to her boss's right, Tommy said to him, "I shot a man yesterday, Artie. I killed him. I never meant to kill anyone. It was awful."

"I'm sure it was, but…"

"It was and still is. I never thought it would be fun, y' know, like shooting at paper targets is fun, haha bang bang you're dead. But no, it's not fun, Artie. I didn't sleep well last night. I had nightmares."

Arthur realized that he hadn't accurately judged the extent of his little brother's upset. He cast aside his own concerns for the moment, got out of his chair and went around to perch on the edge of the desk nearest Tommy and gave his knee a reassuring squeeze. Marge didn't move from the spot where she had been standing behind her boss, but the look on her face reminded Tommy of someone whose favorite teddy bear had just had its little red tongue pulled off.

Though it was a struggle, Tommy tried to maintain a charitable attitude toward his brother and Marge. What a pair, those two, constantly teasing him and ragging at him about his little failures. He couldn't deny, though, at that moment their concern for him was genuine.

Artie returned to the chair behind his desk and Tommy stood to finally remove his parka. A button on the left sleeve of his sport coat was snagged in the sleeve of the parka; Marge came around to help.

Artie said, "Hold up on that, Marge. He'll need to be wearing his parka where he's going. It's cold outside."

"Why? Where am I going?"

"You're going home for a few days rest, a week, maybe. With pay of course. Don't look so surprised, you know the procedure as well as I do. You're on administrative leave until a hearing board rules your shooting justified."

Rest was the last thing Tommy needed, though he wasn't sure what it was he did need.

He said, "But, a week? You've got the police report right there in front of you. The M.E.'s report might be ready now, too." Tommy knew that the M.E.'s report would be delayed until the corpse was identified, and he knew that hadn't happened yet, but he decided not to mention that. "You could hold the hearing this afternoon or tomorrow morning."

* * *

Artie momentarily struggled to hold his tongue and simply stared at his brother. He wasn't angry, Tommy could tell as much. He knew very well what anger looked like on his big brother's face, and this time he could tell Artie wasn't angry. Nor was it the What-have-you-got-yourself-into-this-time look. No, this time it was a look as if he had just heard the punch line of a joke. The lower half of his face got the joke, but the upper half of his face didn't. Artie felt helpless and incredulous, sardonic and sorry, all at once.

That look reflected Arthur's angst to inform Tommy of what was to be. Neither Arthur nor any of the assistant D.A.s would be presiding over the hearing, In fact, Artie had recused them all, most notably himself, and that the Police Commissioner had agreed to appoint Captain Barancovich of the Internal Affairs Division to preside.

"You know the Baran, don't you, Tommy? I remember you telling me you did. He's an okay guy, isn't he? A real straight shooter, right?"

"Jeez. Do I know Barancovich? Everybody in the cops knows Paul Barancovich is the toughest s.o.b. in I.A. What'd I do to deserve him? All I did was defend myself."

Marge said, "In that case, what's to worry? It'll look great, you being exonerated by the toughest cop on the force. And everyone, especially the powers that be in the community, will be able to say that justice was served."

Tommy couldn't deny it. It would look great for the D.A.'s re-election campaign.

Tommy stood. He decided to leave before he got any angrier at his brother and Marge. But he couldn't help saying, "There was a point yesterday, right after the shooting, when I realized it was the worst possible time for it to have happened. It being an election year, and all. But I dismissed that. You'll have to excuse me, both of you, but I wasn't thinking about how it would look to the voters when that joker, whoever he was, came at me with a knife."

Artie said, "If that's the way it went down, nobody would expect you to."

"No," Marge said, "and…"

"Whaddaya mean, if that's the way it went down?"

"I mean, it's funny," Artie said, shaking his head in disbelief. "What kind of nut would do a crazy thing like that, charge into a drawn gun? That is the way it went down? Tommy?"

"Well…yes."

"Tom Murdoch?" This wasn't Tommy's brother asking, it was Arthur P. Murdoch, the Allegheny County District Attorney.

"Yes, what's in the report is what happened. I don't…I don't tell lies." Is leaving something out the same as a lie? "I don't understand why you recused your entire department. This could've been over and done with in no time."

In a soft voice meant to calm his brother Artie said, "No, bro. Unfortunately it couldn't be over in no time. You didn't just kill a man, you killed a black man. That complicates matters nowadays, no matter what the circumstances."

Marge said, "Imagine how it would look, Tommy, you being the District Attorney's brother, if we hurried up and dealt with it ourselves. How would it look to people like the Reverend Jesse Jackson or Al Sharpton? How would it look to the people of Pittsburgh if the headlines read…" She paused to draw them in the air. "After quick hearing, D.A. Arthur Murdoch exonerates his little brother. How do you think it would look? Appearances matter, Tommy."

"And black lives matter, too, don't they?"

Margie put enough pressure on Tommy's shoulders to force him back down in his chair. She kept her hands on his shoulders, hoping it would give him some comfort. Though she knew Tommy appreciated the impact of his actions on the upcoming election, it mattered a lot less than a man's death. Tommy didn't care whether his victim was black or white, only that he was dead, and that the death was on him.

She said, "By that I mean, too many white cops have killed too many black men lately, Tommy. That's what I mean; nothing more, nothing less. Not your fault, dear, but there it is."

Artie seconded Marge with an emphatic nod of his head, then gestured with a hand in such a way that Tommy realized he was being dismissed. His brother and Marge had a department to run; they had bigger fish to fry than him. He was ordered home for R & R until his hearing, the time and place of which he would be duly notified. Goodbye and good luck.

* * *

Tommy felt unfairly put upon; it felt like a lump in his throat that was hard to swallow. He intended on his way out of the building to talk the whole matter over with Mayor Caliguiri, but it had started to rain and the elementary students were milling about on the portico waiting, he assumed, for their buses to return them to school.

Look at the crazy man talking to a statue.

Instead, he turned up his coat collar against the rain and headed for his car.

CHAPTER 6

Tommy had just climbed behind the wheel of the Dodge Dart when his cell phone buzzed. He was surprised a cell signal could penetrate all the concrete two levels below the Public Safety Building, but it had. Caller ID said, Callahan. She was calling from her personal cell phone.

She said, "Hey, Murdoch, there's good news, and if you take me to dinner tonight, I'll share it with you."

The invitation in her voice sent a zing of electricity down his spine. Officer Callahan had been bold and brassy the day Tommy first met her—Was it only yesterday? It felt like forever ago—but so had he been brassy and bold, bolder than he'd ever been. Maybe she had just been following his lead. The warmth in her voice now, possibly distorted a bit by their cell phones, took him by surprise.

He stammered, "Well, uh…"

"Gee, Murdoch," she said, the brass back in her voice. "How do you expect to make out with a girl if you don't at least treat her to dinner?"

"Don't get me wrong, I want to, I really do. It's just, I've been so preoccupied … you know."

"Preoccupied, yeah, I understand. Okay, I'll tell you the news, but don't think it's for free. I still want that dinner."

She told him that a fingerprint ID report came back from the FBI in Washington. "Your perp," she said, "had a criminal record that reaches all the way to Saint Louis. Lots of petty thefts, B&Es, car-jackings, assaults. Seems your boy had a mean temper."

My boy, Tommy thought. *All of a sudden he's my boy?*

He couldn't help saying, "Did my shooting him make him my boy?" His anger was understandable, but at her? He apologized for it.

"Forget it, I understand."

She went on, careful not to call the perp his perp, to point out that the perp's having a record of robberies and violent assaults had the effect of taking a little of the pressure off of Tommy.

She said, "Not even that I.A. son of a bitch, Barancovich, can fault you for shooting him.

"By the way," she continued, "his name is Willams."

"Who?"

"Who do you think? The perp. His name is Odell Willams."

"Williams?"

"No, Willams. W-i-l-l-a-m-s. Odell Willams."

Tommy said the only thing that came to mind. "Never heard of him."

*   *   *

Tommy said to himself, "So, I have a dinner date." Even the sound of it pleased him as the words echoed around in the confines of his parked car.

Then he said, "I have a girl friend." That pleased him, too, but he wondered if it weren't premature. He tended to be premature when it came to women.

Just as much as he liked the idea of a girl friend, he liked the idea of a hot shower and maybe a BLT on toast for lunch, and most of all, an afternoon nap. He was more than a little bit weary. He remembered what the instructors in Law Enforcement at CCAC had said about the exhausting effects of shock, both physical and emotional. It was not yet noon, he'd been awake no more than three or four hours, yet he was as weary as if he had just slouched away from work after a double shift. He turned the key that woke up the Dodge Dart's ancient engine. He wound his way out from under the Public Safety Building and aimed for home.

CHAPTER 7

District Attorney Arthur Murdoch, his wife Nina—Tommy's sister-in-law—and their two young daughters, Edie and Madison— Tommy's nieces—lived in a huge old mansion on Mayfield, a tree-lined avenue that squatted on the border between the Oakland and Squirrel Hill neighborhoods. The mansion once served as residence for the president of Carnegie Mellon University; it was a stone's throw from that university and within sight of the City's other major university, the University of Pittsburgh, with its forty-five story Cathedral of Learning. The mansion's one hundredth birthday was celebrated nearly two decades ago. It was a grand pile, with a half-circle driveway approaching the front entrance and a second driveway with a port cochere at the north side entrance. It had many working fireplaces and chimneys, and behind the house, it had a servant family's quarters above the four-carriage garage. Arthur had those servants' quarters remodeled as an apartment for his little brother.

Tommy loved his carriage house apartment. It was a terrific suite of fully furnished rooms: a bedroom with a full en suite bath and a window that caught the early morning sunlight, whenever the sun chose to grace a western Pennsylvania morning; also it had a combination office/study with shelves for his books, and a kitchenette that was the perfect size for a bachelor who ate out most of the time. All thanks to Artie, who arranged it all.

* * *

Tommy truly believed that his Mom, on her deathbed, had pleaded with Arthur—she never called him Artie, always it was Arthur—to look after his little brother. Like a precious baby doll that is coveted for years by a child before she actually receives it, Tommy, having come along after his mother's two life-threatening miscarriages, was her favorite child. But she harbored no illusions about his capabilities. Tommy was not a witness to any such deathbed scene, but he believed it had taken place, and he thought he knew what Arthur had said in reply: "You don't have to ask, Mom. I always have looked after him and I always will."

And, much to Tommy's chagrin, he always had and always did—typical big brother, always ready to fight Tommy's battles for him. Not that he needed to fight all that often. Tommy was a big, tough kid, able to handle himself.

Most of the time. Not always. There had been an occasion or two when, in spite of his size, Tommy was bullied in the elementary school play yard by a gang of tough boys. Artie appeared seemingly out of nowhere with the extra pair of fists Tommy needed. It was a different kind of battle when the Dean of Admissions at CCAC said that Thomas's high school grades were inadequate for admission. Artie stepped in there, too, that time with a bit of political influence. Yet another time when Tommy got arrested for getting into a fist fight with a noisy, half-drunk wise guy at the bar of the Duquesne Club. Tommy straightened a few of the wise guy's crooked teeth and un-straightened his nose. Artie had to arrange for Tommy's bail. At the time Tommy didn't think Artie minded appearing in magistrate's court at two a.m. Later he wasn't so sure.

* * *

Nina Delaney Murdoch, Arthur's wife and Tommy's sister-in-law, was a beautiful woman, fair-haired, fair-complexioned and fair minded. She and Artie met when they were both students at University of Pennsylvania Law School. Now Nina was a top earner at a prestigious firm while managing—with a little hired help—to be the epitome of a helicopter mom at the same time. When Tommy was first introduced to her, he thought Nina was a bit of an ice queen, but he was wrong about that. Nina made it clear to him right after she and Artie were married that their home was Tommy's home, that there would always be a place for him at their table, that he didn't have to eat another meal at a diner, if he didn't want to.

Nina was the closest thing to a real sister a person could wish for.

But a person had to be careful what he wished for. Were big sisters anything like big brothers? Tommy didn't know. Were big sisters smothering and over protective, like mother hens? He had enough of that with his brother, Arthur.

After a while Tommy began to feel as if Nina had begun to lose patience with him; felt she wanted for herself and her daughters the time and effort her husband dedicated to looking after him. Nina was a truly good person, Tommy was convinced of that, so he knew she wouldn't be happy to know that he sensed that about her, but whenever Tommy graced the family with his presence, he detected little things in Nina's behavior that made him think he had over-stayed his welcome. As if he had promised to visit for a week, but on the eighth day, he was still there. Or was he wrong about that, too?

* * *

The rain had stopped and the sun was peeking out from behind drifting clouds, causing steam from wet pavements to rise like exhaled breath. As Tommy pulled into a parking slot beneath his apartment in the carriage house, his nieces, Edie and Madison, were on the lawn tossing a rubber ball back and forth with Bobbi in the so-called soup. Bobbi chased from one girl to the other, crowing joyfully as beagles do. As

Tommy closed the garage door, he looked up toward the house. He saw that, true to Nina's role as helicopter mom, she had a watchful eye on the game from her bedroom window. They exchanged waves.

Climbing the stairs to his apartment was a struggle—his knees, stiff with fatigue, protested having to bend. Stress had exhausted him. He was looking forward to a nap before his date with Officer Callahan, and at the same time hoping not to repeat the dream he had suffered through the previous night. In it Tommy kept shooting and shooting and shooting until his assailant finally exploded into a million bloody smithereens.

Once inside the apartment, he decided to forego a shower; decided to forego a BLT on toast, as well. Skipped directly to the nap. Fear of repeating the dream slowed his undressing considerably, and when he finally crawled into bed, he fell into a predictably troubled sleep.

*   *   *

That evening Arthur, surprised and thrilled that, for once, his brother had taken his advice about something, in this case about getting some rest, Arthur loaned him the use of the family's white BMW sedan. Tommy tooled it through the downtown and took the 9th Street bridge over the Allegheny River to the North Side. Callahan lived in an efficiency apartment on the third floor of a multi-story building on Federal

Street, near the old Buhl Planetarium. He rode up the elevator and knocked on her door.

Officer Callahan opened the door. After a few moments hunting for his tongue and stammering, Tommy told her how nice she looked. Once his Mom had advised him to always tell a girl how nice she looked, even if she didn't. But Officer Callahan really really did. She was wearing black slacks and a silky, long-sleeved white blouse with black polka dots. Simple but elegant, he thought, well chosen, and on her, very sexy.

She approved of the Western look he had chosen, too: pressed jeans, a green corduroy sport coat with a gray shirt and string tie. He was a hunk.

"Except for these," she said. "Little stress wrinkles." She reached out and touched him lightly in the middle of his forehead, between his eyebrows. To Tommy it felt like a kiss.

She retrieved a black leather jacket from a closet, he helped her on with it, and they headed out.

CHAPTER 8

Tommy was surprised to discover that the James Street Tavern was near enough to Callahan's building that walking there would have been quicker than finding a parking spot. The parking lot full on a weeknight? Then again, the Tavern was the favorite venue of Pittsburgh's jazz music fans. It was once just a blue-collar neighborhood hangout. Now it had a combination restaurant and bar on the ground level, and at the basement level it had a performance stage, a crowded area of cocktail tables and a postage-stamp sized dance floor. Tommy and Officer Callahan took a table on the ground level so they could eat and talk and still hear the music as it drifted up from below. That night a piano trio was playing standard tunes in the West Coast 'cool' style.

After they ordered beers and took a little time just silently admiring present company, Tommy admitted that he had no idea what her first name was. What a faux pas, his Mom would be disappointed in him but maybe not surprised.

She thought a moment. "If I tell you what it is, will you promise never to use it?"

He wrinkled his brow.

"Okay, it's Elizabeth. My Dad used to call me Liz 2. My mother was either Liz 1 or Lizzie. But I want you to continue calling me Callahan. Promise?"

Tommy didn't see what was wrong with Elizabeth, but...her choice. He nodded in agreement.

"Not that there's anything wrong with Elizabeth or Liz." She leaned over the table toward him, waved him closer. She whispered, "It's just, it gives me a little zing, y' know what I mean, whenever I hear you call me Callahan."

Tommy said over and over, "Callahan, Callahan, Callahan. " He watched her to see what a zing looked like. He thought he saw her butt pop up an inch or two off her chair. They both laughed.

There were two TV screens mounted on the wall above the bar, both showing sports events with the sound muted: a basketball game on one, Steelers football highlights on the other. The bar, separated from the dining area by a clear glass partition, was crowded. The stools along the length of the bar were all occupied, with standees clustered among them. The TVs were ignored; there was much gab and high-pitched laughter, mostly in hushed tones in deference to the music. This, after all, was a listening place.

* * *

Callahan and Tommy were both served drafts of

IC Lite in old fashioned pilsner glasses. Callahan took a sip of hers, put the glass down in front of her, moistened a fingertip and ran circles around the rim. She was circling a subject she was reluctant to broach.

She said, addressing her beer to avoid Tommy's eyes, that she and her partner were out of the precinct house during every duty shift, answering all the 911 calls coming into Division 4. They were out on the streets, armed and ready for anything. Doing just about everything from rescuing pet cats out of trees to scraping frozen homeless people off the sidewalks—more often the cats in Division 4, but the homeless sometimes. She was no old timer by any stretch of the imagination, but she was no rookie, either. She'd been around a little while.

"But I've never," she said. "Y' know? I've never."

No, she hadn't ever, Tommy thought. Division 4 covered one of the most upscale neighborhoods in the city. As long as she was stationed at Division 4 it wasn't likely that she would ever have to.

He said, "You've never shot anyone. I thought not, most cops haven't. I hadn't either, until…you know."

"I need you to tell me, if it's not too upsetting."

"You wanna know, what? What it feels like?"

"If it's not too upsetting."

Tommy took a swallow of beer. "There's not much to tell, really.

You pull the trigger and the weapon recoils in your hand, it's like being kicked awake from a dream. Your ears are ringing, the air stinks of burnt cordite and faintly tastes of gun oil. Somebody is lying there dead and your only thought isn't rational. You feel massive-chest-ed, with the power of life and death in your hands. God-like, almost. You don't just feel like a god, you are a god. But that exhilarating feeling doesn't last long. You notice your knees are knocking, they're like jelly, and your legs are complaining, hey, do I have to keep holding you up? There's a quaking in the pit of your stomach, like any second you're gonna puke. Then you know for a fact: you are a god, alright, and you know for sure what a lousy job being God is."

Tommy paused to think it over. "That's pretty much it."

Callahan read the anguish on his face and was sorry she had asked. She reached over and took his hand. She said, "I shouldn't have asked, I'm so sorry, Hon. You're not happy about what happened, anybody can see that. But what choice did you have? It's not as if the perp gave you much choice, right? It wasn't your fault he decided to lunge at you."

Tommy wondered what she had done to her eyes, something with mascara, he guessed, though he knew nothing about such things as mascara. But she looked delicious. Those eyes of hers were pulling him in; he couldn't have resisted even if he had wanted to, and he didn't want to. And her bosom looked so inviting and comforting. Oh, to rest his head on her bosom, as he used to on Mom's.

He said, "I wish I was sure it wasn't my fault. I wish, but all I can think of since I pulled the trigger is, I wish I hadn't."

They were interrupted by a goateed string-bean of a man of indeterminate age. He was wearing jeans slashed at the knees, a red wool overshirt and a striped apron. A silver stud pierced one nostril.

He asked, "Y'uns wanna hear t'night's specials?" They didn't, but there was no stopping him. "We got a hearty pea soup with limas and garbanzo beans. And the special burger of the day is a three-quarter pounder with provolone, mushrooms and carmelized unyums." They both ordered the burger special. "Would y'uns like the soup?"

"Not for me, thanks," Tommy said.

Callahan said, "My mother taught me never to order anything with beans when I'm on a date."

The server went away chuckling. As soon as he was gone, she took hold of Tommy's hand again.

He said, "The perp, whatsisname? Willams. He threatened us with the knife, me and Bobbi. That part is true. So I showed him my H&K."

"So he lunged at you, ready to stab you. Hard to believe, but that's how it went down, right?"

"Well…almost." Tommy turned away from her, changing his mind about saying anything more, then changed his mind again. He needed to tell someone. If he could tell anyone, he felt he could tell Callahan. "The perp said, well, the gist of what he said was, he was going to go away as fast as he could."

"But he didn't."

"No, he didn't. I… I told him that he'd better get a move on…"

The little boy was leery of telling his mommy, but he'd peed in his pants.

"I told him that if he didn't make it quick, I was going to put some lead into that big fat black ass of his."

Callahan recoiled.

"Something wrong?"

She recovered quickly. "No, no, go on."

Having finally told the whole story lifted a ton of weight off Tommy's chest, but not the guilt. "I goaded him, that's when he lunged at me."

"You didn't know he would do that. What a temper he must've had. How could you have known?"

"Yeah, but I shouldn't have said that. It's not like me to say that kinda thing."

"Look, since it troubles you so much, I'm glad you told me. But don't tell anybody else, Tommy, not even your brother. Let it be our secret, okay?" She squeezed his hand for emphasis. He nodded. "But still. Goading him by saying, your big fat black ass, wouldn't cause a person to do something as crazy as lunging at a drawn gun. If anyone should know, I should."

Tommy looked at her, 'Why?' written all over his face.

"Jeez, Tommy. You don't get skin the color of mine by drinking Starbucks lattes. I'm half black. My ass is half black, so I should know. You're surprised. Not too surprised, I hope. Dad, Eamon Callahan was his name, boy, was he Irish! He was Irish through and through, but mother was African-American and proud of it. If that makes any difference to you…"

What a time for their burger platters to arrive. The server carried them on wooden paddles. He said, "Bone Apatee," and departed.

While Callahan was spreading Heinz's best on her fries, Tommy was thinking.

He wondered aloud, "I'm all white, you're half black. What would our kids be, vanilla fudge ripple?"

Startled at first, but then she laughed.

* * *

Later that night they were parked in front of Calla-han's building with the BMW's motor running to keep the temperature up and the windows from steaming over. Tommy found himself wishing they were seated in one of the Buicks or Oldsmobiles his father used to own. Those huge old gas guzzlers had bench seats and gear shift levers on the steering column. In the BMW no matter how they shifted around in the bucket seats, it was impossible to get as close to her as he wanted to.

"The jazz music was really nice, wasn't it?" Callahan said.

"It was. I love it when you can watch the players passing the musical ideas around from one guy to the other. The way their faces light up when somebody does something unusual. I only wish I understood music the way they do."

"I know what you mean. Sometimes when I'm listening to jazz, I feel like an outsider."

Callahan changed the subject.

"Tommy, that time when we met on the stairs in Division 4. Remember? You and Bobbi were going up and I was coming down? I knew right away that you liked me. I could read it on your face like I was reading a page of USA Today. It was that obvious."

"I'm sure. I can't resist a woman in uniform."

"Get serious. I kinda felt the same way, but don't you think talking like you did before, about our children, is, to be frank, way out of line?"

"I wanted to get my order in early. Okay, okay, I'll be serious. I was never good at judging the appropriateness of things. Mom always had to reprimand me for embarrassing people with my big mouth." He shrugged. "I didn't mean to embarrass you. I'm sorry."

"Apology accepted. I didn't mind all that much. But you have to realize there are times when it's better to leave things unsaid. Think them all you want, but you need to keep them to yourself. Until they're appropriate, I mean. Y' know?"

"Like what I said to the perp? I know, mum's the word, not even to my brother or Marge Tangretti. But I admit I'm not real clear on why."

While Callahan pondered how to answer him, she looked up at the little lamp she had left on in her third floor window. It had an inviting golden glow in the darkness.

She said, "You think what you said to the perp and why you said it make all the difference. And maybe they do make all the difference, but only to you. In your mind. To everyone else, what you said and why you said it make no difference at all, really. They're moot, as the lawyers say, beside the point, a mere complication."

"You think?"

"Yes, I definitely do. And this being an election year, the last thing your brother needs right now is a complication."

"Huh. I thought that way, too, right after the fact. I

mean, right after I shot him, I thought, 'This is going to mean a change in my routine for a couple of days, nothing more.' That's while I was still a god, high on having the power of life and death in me. But when I came down from the high, I thought, 'This is liable to become a shit storm for my brother.'"

* * *

Saying good night at her door, Tommy asked Callahan if he could kiss her good night. She replied, "Okay, but just one."

But as if they were eating salted peanuts or M&Ms, they couldn't restrict themselves to just one.

CHAPTER 9

Next morning Tommy awoke hugging his pillow. Without looking at the clock radio on the nightstand beside his bed, simply by noting the position of the light from the window projected onto the bedroom walls, he knew it was approximately six a.m. He had been so physically and mentally drained when he arrived home the night before, he had forgotten to close the blind.

He untangled himself from the bed clothes, clambered out of bed and went to the window. He peered out on one of those November mornings that western Pennsylvanians are unfortunate to have grown used to: the air penetratingly damp, the sky oatmeal-gray in color with swift-moving, ominous lumps of cloud. The cold, hardwood floor stung his bare feet.

He wasn't sure—he never was—if the sounds of his waking had roused Bobbi, or if Bobbi's moving around in her crate had roused him. No matter. He showered and dressed in jeans, a long-sleeved plaid shirt, winter vest and a Steelers ball cap. He fed Bobbi and, as usual after her meal, walked her around the neighborhood. Thoughts of Odell Willams and the shooting made it a chore instead of a joy. Then he thought of feeding himself. He returned Bobbi to her crate and drove the Dodge Dart—it felt like a wounded warrior compared to the BMW Artie let him use last night—to the diner on Baum Boulevard.

* * *

Of course Callahan played a major role in last night's dream. Gentle, warm-hearted soul that she was despite her chosen profession of police officer, Tommy thought she would be pleased to learn that her appearance in his dreams the previous night had restrained him considerably—he hadn't pumped nearly as much lead into Odell Willams as he had in the previous two nights' dreams. Still, Tommy was a confused bag of conflicting emotions. Neither the stroll with Bobbi in the early morning chill nor a stack of buttermilk pancakes slathered in creamery butter, maple syrup and a triple rasher of bacon—crisp, the way he liked it—were able to calm him. He had never before been on leave from work, and for him idleness was anathema. On top of that, he was walking around without the weight of his H&K holstered snugly against his back, and although he felt naked without it, he wasn't sure he wanted to carry ever again. He felt greatly relieved to have survived a deadly attack, but guilty at having taken a life in the process. He felt regret at causing a complication for his brother in an election year, and on top of everything else, he was in love. Head over heels, ass over tea cups in love.

* * *

Tommy stared at the dregs at the bottom of his second cup of coffee, and was considering a third cup. On the muted TV a local show, Good Morning Pittsburgh, was running highlights of last weekend's high school football games. Waves of color ebbed and flowed across the screen. Tommy's mind leapt from the colorful football images to his pal, Mickey Skruggs.

It was an indication of just how preoccupied Tommy had been the previous two days that he hadn't thought of Mickey before this. But now that he had, he knew his friend Mick was the one man in the world he could talk freely to about the ugliness that spewed from his mouth at Odell Willams. He paid his tab, including the usual 15% tip for the counter lady, and left the diner.

He drove his Dart onto the Parkway, crossed over the Allegheny River via the Fort Duquesne Bridge, and once he was on the North Side he headed for his alma mater, CCAC, the Community College of Allegheny County. As he passed PNC Park, the home field of the Pittsburgh Pirates, he was amused to think he could hit the CCAC with a baseball thrown from PNC Park; that is, he could hit it from there if he had one hell of a better throwing arm than he actually had.

He drove around back of the school's Athletic Field House and parked nearest the players' entrance and managers' offices.

* * *

Michael Skruggs was Equipment Supervisor for the entire CCAC Athletic Department. Tommy first met him when he, Tommy, was a student majoring in Law Enforcement Studies. Tommy, 5 foot 10 inches tall and stockily-built, convinced himself that he could earn a spot on the basketball squad. He tried and of course failed—he was the epitome of the white boy who couldn't jump. Or shoot. Still, he enjoyed the easy camaraderie of the Athletic Department, so he volunteered to hang around and help with equipment. He became Mickey Skruggs's chief aide. The guys on the teams dubbed Tommy the vice president in charge of jock straps. They teased in a good-natured way, so Tommy didn't mind.

When he had earned an associate degree and went on to the Police Academy, Tommy no longer had time to help Mickey with equipment, but the two men remained friends. Mickey was not only his friend, but also his confidant.

Though the two men were as different as night and day, pun intended since Skruggs was a black man and several years older than Tommy, they had one sure thing in common: they both had super-achieving older brothers.

At the time, Arthur Murdoch was a successful prosecutor in the D.A.'s Office and beginning to be a somebody in the Democratic Party, and Mickey's brother, Charlie Skruggs, played tight end for the

L.A. Rams and had a few good years in the NFL in the early 2000s. The after-effects of several concussions forced his retirement. Charlie Skruggs was the same kind of loving but controlling, overbearing to the point of smothering, big brother as was Arthur. Tommy and Mickey used to meet over beers weekly at a tavern across from the school and commiserate about being pushed around by their big brothers. The meetings had become sporadic lately, the last one being five, no, six months ago. Tommy had been busy and he supposed Mickey had been, too. Tommy was eager to see him.

* * *

Tommy used the players' entrance, crossed the widths of two basketball courts and cut through the men's locker room. Off to the left he could hear the familiar sounds of clanking metal and grunting men coming from the weight room. The air was redolent of B.O., of course, but in the equipment area, along with the B.O. were the rattle of clothes tumbling in dryers and the smell of Clorox—to Tommy it felt like home.

Both halves of the Dutch door to Mickey's office were closed and locked. Mick had taken the day off, he figured.

Stupid of you not to have called first, could have saved yourself a trip, he could hear Artie saying, his voice dripping with scorn.

* * *

Tommy re-traced his steps through the locker room and one basketball court; on the second court the men of the varsity team were running through routine give-and-go drills—routine to them, Tommy thought. They never had been routine to him, with his two left feet. He was fascinated to watch them pass and cut to the basket, pass and cut to the basket, long arms, long legs, pass and cut to the basket.

Someone called, "You lookin' for somebody?"

It was a young woman pushing a wheeled laundry cart; she was headed with the cart toward the washing machines and dryers. Tommy figured her for a work-study student. She wore a modified afro streaked with green dye to match her green scrubs. It was years since Tommy had worked there; he was a stranger. The young woman's large brown eyes showed caution until Mickey's name was mentioned. She visibly relaxed.

She said, "The Mick is over at Saint Al's getting nuked."

Tommy was stunned when he realized she was referring to Saint Aloysius Hospital. "Mick's in the hospital?"

"Ain't heard of any placed called Saint Al's that ain't the hospital. Those treatments knock the shit out of Mick. I don't expect to see him around here for least two, three days."

"What treatments? What's wrong with The Mick?"

"You don't know? I thought you said you was a friend of his. He got a case of the Big C," she said, shaking her head, her eyes seeing the poor man into his grave.

Tommy felt as if he had been slugged on the chest, right over his heart. He managed to take a breath, managed to ask if she happened to know what floor he was on or his room number.

She said, "He won't be allowed no visitors, his brother maybe, but you ain't family."

The way she said you irritated Tommy. He knew what she meant: him, a white man.

"The hell with that," he said, thinking he would flash his badge if he had to. Not realizing that his badge along with his H&K were in somebody's desk drawer at Division 4. He hustled toward the exit.

Chapter 10

As the crow flies UPMC Mercy Hospital, sitting as it does on the eastern edge of downtown, was a lot closer to CCAC than Saint Aloysius. Saint Al's, as almost everyone called it, was on the South side and CCAC was on the North side, with the traffic congestion of downtown Pittsburgh forming an impenetrable wall between the two. But Tommy wasn't a crow and Saint Al's, against all logic, was actually closer, not in distance but in travel time. He knew this because once the Mick had to drive him to the emergency room with a gusher of a nose bleed after Tommy had collided with a rebounding basketball. So with the help of two bridges, one over the Allegheny River and one over the Monongahela, and using Fort Duquesne Boulevard to circumvent downtown's so-called Golden Triangle, Tommy arrived at Saint Al's in less than ten minutes.

On his way across the pedestrian bridge that spanned Worth Street and connected the 3rd level of the parking garage to the 2nd floor of Saint Al's, Tommy received a cell phone call from the D.A.'s Office. Artie himself. Checking up on me, Tommy thought, since it was Artie instead of Marge.

Artie said, "Where are you, Dickhead? Staying out of trouble, I hope."

"Screw you, Artie."

"And you too, dear brother."

When the pleasantries were concluded, Artie got down to business with the reason for the call: the hearing into the shooting of Odell Willams would take place at 10 a.m. on Monday morning in the media room of the Public Safety Building. It was now official that it would be conducted by Capt. Barancovich of Internal Affairs.

"Why the media room, for Chrissake? They're making a circus out of this, aren't they?"

"Calm down, bro. It's not shaping up to be a circus, at all. Just the opposite. But think of it this way: We're in a poker game, and we think the best way to win the pot is to show our hand, every card, to everybody sitting at the table."

Who's we, Tommy wondered.

"You know, Tommy, the shooting of a black man by a white cop can't help being a big deal as far as the public, and the media, are concerned. But don't worry. Even though you stepped right in it, you'll come out with no shit on your shoe. God willing."

"I'm not a cop."

"A County Detective, same thing."

"Leave it to me, right, to shoot someone in an

election year. But tell me, Artie," Tommy said, mentally cursing all politicians, every last one of them, including his brother, "If there's no shit on my shoe, what's that I smell?"

* * *

Bill Murphy, Hospital Security, dressed in dark blue uniform trousers and contrasting pale blue shirt, was trying to make himself useful at the entrance to Saint Al's. For instance, Murphy would hold the door for anyone who didn't look capable of doing it him or herself. He was no fount of information, Murphy. But if he didn't know the answer to a question put to him, he at least knew how to direct people to the information booth. Murphy had been on the County Police Force when Tommy first joined that Force and had retired shortly after Tommy left for the D.A.'s Office. Murphy recognized Tommy immediately, and Tommy remembered him, too. Murphy was not the brightest bulb in the lamp and he had never advanced beyond uniformed patrolman. But as it turned out, Murphy proved capable of holding the door for Tommy even though Tommy was capable of doing it himself, and although Murphy didn't know anyone named Skruggs, he knew that most cases of the Big C were being treated on the 6th floor. And he knew where the elevator could be found.

* * *

Saint Al's used to be the City's foremost Catholic hospital, and the excellent nursing care provided by the nuns and their devotion to duty were legendary among Pittsburghers old enough to remember back then. Exactly when that changed Tommy didn't know, but it had. There were no nuns in sight when he stepped off the elevator on 6. He noticed only a trace of alcohol in the air that he could taste as well as smell, and a fearful silence that chilled him.

An inquiry at the nurse's station eventually got Tommy the number of Mickey's room; it was 618. But his reward for asking was a sour look from a young woman named Kenda—first or last name? Her ID tag didn't specify. She was dressed like all the other nurses on the floor, in blue scrubs. A butterfly tattoo on her left bicep was Kenda's flair of fashion. To Tommy, she didn't look old enough to be out of high school.

Kenda said, "You're not his brother, he's...uh, taller than you."

"He's black is what his brother is. I'm his white friend, his good white friend. It's not illegal."

"I didn't mean... aw, look. Mr. Skruggs is awful weak, and his immune system, well, you'll have to wear one of those yellow paper gowns. You'll find them near the door to his room. Like I said, he's awful weak. Try not to stay too long, okay?"

Tommy was tempted to ask how long was too long, but he figured Kenda wouldn't appreciate it.

She would aim another one of those sour looks at him. Besides, she seemed to care about Mickey. Maybe she didn't deserve any shit from him. He promised not to stay too long, thanked her and walked up the hall reading the numbers on the doors, searching for 618.

*   *   *

Tommy entered Mickey's room and looked around while he struggled into a yellow paper gown. He hadn't been in very many hospital rooms, but he didn't have to have been in many to recognize this one as pretty standard: it was rectangular, with a bathroom to his immediate right and a large window in the wall opposite the door. There was a standard hospital bed, unmade and at the moment empty. A large reclining chair was turned in such a way that its occupant could look out the window and see the entire Southside as it meandered down from the bluff on which Saint Al's was perched. From Saint Al's on the top of the bluff all the way down to the Monongahela river.

Mickey was slouched in the recliner with his back to the door, an IV hanger on one side of him with a line running to his left arm. His large round head was covered down to the ears with a wooly-looking do rag.

Without making an effort to turn around, Mickey said, "What's it like out there today, nurse? I can see it's windy, but is it cold?" Then he added dreamily, "Some view, this. Man, if only I could fly like a bird, I could fly all the way down to the Allegheny River."

"It's not a nurse, it's me, Mick." Tommy said. "And for your information, that's not the Allegheny, it's the Mon."

Mickey struggled to maneuver the recliner around, but the chair was too heavy for him; he was losing the struggle. Tommy hurried over to help. When Mickey finally faced his visitor, Tommy nearly fainted. The strapping bruiser he knew as Mickey Skruggs had shrunk to half his former size. He had not only lost weight, he had lost substance. The flesh hung from his bones like drapes, and his skin, which Tommy used to joke was the color of peanut butter, was now gray.

It took Skruggs a few beats to speak, as if the very act took considerably more energy than he had. When he finally did speak, he said, "Hey…Thomas. My man."

He made an effort to get up but couldn't manage that, either. Tommy was glad when Mickey gave up trying. The gray workout suit he was wearing might have been his own, but he was swimming in it, as if he had put on his brother Charlie's by mistake. Had he stood up out of the chair, his pants would have fallen down to his ankles.

Tommy said, "Stay put, Mick. I'll sit here on the bed." When he was seated and had turned his friend's chair so he was facing him, Tommy said, "You'll forgive me for saying, Mick, but you look like shit. What's going on? The girl that works for you over at CCAC, she said they were nuking you."

Skruggs wheezed. "With the green hair? That's LaVonna. Not the swiftest bird in the flock, by a long shot. A good worker, though. Not good as you..." He paused to breathe. "...Thomas, but good. No, they ain't nuking me, they're squirting poison into me." He showed Tommy the line running chemo into the vein in his arm. "Some mighty mean kinda poison."

"Where is it? The Big C, I mean, where... you know."

"Somewhere in here," Skruggs said, indicating his belly. "Somewhere in my guts. Tell me again what your Jew half calls it. I forget the word."

"Kishkis," Tommy said.

"That's a fun word, kishkis, yeah, that's it. And how about your Irish half, what do they call it?"

"I'm not sure. Maybe spalpeens."

"I'm black on both sides, we call it chitlins. I got the Big C of the Chitlins."

They had hardly begun to laugh when Skruggs groaned and bent over in the chair. Tommy was too stunned to move, but then he grabbed onto his friend, hoping to take some of the pain.

"Oh, Mick, it hurts, doesn't it? How can I help? What can I do?"

He held tightly to him.

* * *

Nurse Kenda, obviously having seen something on her monitor that she didn't like, rapped on the door and came through. She found her patient in the visitor's desperate grasp. She aimed one of her sour looks at both men. Skruggs managed to assure her that he was all right. The visitor promised to be saying his goodbyes soon. Kenda frowned, but backed out.

After a swallow of water from the glass Tommy handed him and a few breaths, Skruggs recovered to something that resembled normalcy. He returned to the conversation lacking energy but with his usual teasing sense of humor.

Mickey said, "Been a while since I seen you around CCAC. You must a been busy saving the world from all them bad guys out there, huh, Thomas?"

Reading stress on Tommy's face, though, and thinking maybe it was brother trouble again, Skruggs said, "There be something you need to talk over with your old friend, the Mick?"

Or was this, after all, just a social call?

He asked Thomas, "Whatcha call a hospital visit, another of them Jew words?"

"A mitzvah call." Another phrase Tommy had heard his mother use.

His friend Mickey found great humor in Thomas's Jewish side.

* * *

Thomas had suffered as many of nurse Kenda's sour looks as he wished to, so he hurriedly filled his friend in on what had happened to him and Bobbi the other morning on Plainfield Street: that he had shot and killed an attempted mugger, that the mugger's name was Odell Willams and that Willams was a black man. He had thought to discuss with Mick the ugly words he had used to goad Willams, but he decided against doing that. Mickey was too exhausted. He also remembered his promise to Callahan. So his telling of the incident was as terse as the police report, but still it was exactly how it had gone down.

Sort of, Thomas thought.

* * *

By the time Mickey had been brought up to speed on recent events, his gray eyelids were hooded and his big head was drooping toward his lap. He would not be able to hold on to consciousness much longer. He roused himself long enough to ask what Arthur, Thomas's brother, had to say about all this.

Thomas said, "What difference does it make what Artie says?"

"All the difference in the world, Thomas. Listen to him and do whatever he says and you'll be okay."

His reserves of strength were draining, and it showed. Thomas kicked himself for mentioning the whole sordid business. But Mickey went on.

He said, "Take my word, man, when your ass is in a sling, the best medicine is a big brother. Oh, I know, I used to say our big brothers were worse than old ladies, but look at me. Is my ass in a sling, or what? Sheeit! Without brother Charlie, I'd be up shit's creek. He'll be taking me to his place when I'm able to leave here. Someone's gotta take care of me. Who could I rely on but Charlie? I can't hardly wipe my own ass, Thomas. I can't hardly... What would I do..." Skruggs was fading fast. "...without my big..."

Tommy settled him so he wouldn't fall out of the chair and covered him with a blanket from the foot of the bed. He whispered to Mickey, "See you around, old friend."

Not knowing when or if he would see his old friend again, his eyes were blind with tears as he departed the room.

CHAPTER 11

Tommy couldn't get over the fact that his pal Mickey Skruggs's attitude toward his brother Charlie had done a 180 degree turn. The Mick had always chafed under his brother's domineering thumb, now he seemed to be sucking on it. It was true enough that the Big C had him weak as a kitten, and the last thing he needed was to hear Tommy's troubles. At the same time, Tommy knew his friend had served a combat tour in the U.S. Army in the Middle East. He had fought in Operation Desert Storm and had admitted to having dispatched to Hell more than one A-rab enemy at close quarters. So Mickey was more qualified than anyone else to understand what Tommy was feeling about having killed a man.

Illness could have a devastating effect, Tommy knew. So he wondered if Mickey's words, 'Listen carefully to your brother and do what he says?' were actually the Big C talking. Or were they the words of a man whose illness had led him to understand for the first time that some things were more important than other things? This is what Tommy was puzzling over as he retrieved his car from the hospital garage.

* * *

It took less than ten minutes in light traffic to reverse his direction, to cross the Mon into the downtown and to park his Dart under the Public Safety Building. The weather had deteriorated during the hospital visit with Mickey. It felt as if it were too cold to rain, yet too warm to snow. Tommy's ears burned as he walked the distance up Grant Street to the City-County Building, walking with his head down, holding his hat against the wind.

Mayor Caliguiri's business suit fitted him more baggily than present fashion dictated and Tommy thought it was too light in weight for the November chill. He thought it a good thing Hizzoner was made of bronze.

* * *

Passing through security was a breeze, since he had so little metal on him: a few coins and keys—no badge, no H&K. The lunch hour had passed, people were ensconced in their offices, looking busy. The halls were not heavily trafficked. An empty elevator took him up to the D.A.'s suite.

He found Marge eating half of an Italian hoagie at her desk in the outer office. Her day was only half over, but already she looked tired and the charcoal skirt and red blazer she was wearing were beginning to lose their shape. It was at this time of day when her natural hair style, a chaotic mop of dark curls, best reflected her condition.

Marge offered Tommy the other half of her sandwich; he had left his appetite at Saint Al's. He settled for a paper cup of coffee from a thermos she pulled out of the drawer of her desk.

Tommy watched her eat, tapping his foot with impatience. He said, "Well, what's new, what's happening?"

Marge was not about to reply until she had dealt with a mouthful of hoagie. When she was able to, she said, "If you mean around here, I'm having my lunch, as you can see. If by what's happening you mean in the case of the City of Pittsburgh and County of Allegheny v. Odell Willams, deceased, then everything and nothing is happening."

So far no one had claimed the body. The police were still hunting, so far unsuccessfully, for next-of-kin or anyone else, for that matter, who could supply authorities with information as to how or why Odell Willams came from St. Louis, Missouri, the place of his last arrest, to Pittsburgh, PA. What was he doing here besides attempting assault and armed robbery? Nobody admitted to knowing the answer to that or even admitted to knowing him. Which, Marge said, was good. If nobody knew him and nobody even admitted to having met him, nobody might make too big a stink over Tommy's having shot him.

She had other good news for Tommy. The CSI squad had found no evidence at the scene to dispute the facts provided by him in the statement he dictated and signed. And the cops had rapped on every door in the vicinity of the incident in search of anyone who had witnessed the incident. No one had.

Marge said, "Willams is in the fridge at the County Morgue, he's not going anywhere. So, you wanna know what's happening? Until the hearing on Monday morning, nothing. Hopefully."

Tommy decided to speak to his brother to tell him about Mickey Skruggs's cancer. Artie knew Mickey's brother, Charlie, much better than he knew Mickey, but he had met Mickey a few times. Artie would want to know.

He asked, nodding toward the inner door, "Is he in?"

He was not, he had business that kept him at the Courthouse all morning, Marge reported, and would likely be there all afternoon.

"But you needn't worry," she said to reassure him. "If anything crops up that needs seeing to, your brother will see to it. Or I will."

That was precisely what Tommy wished to avoid. Artie shouldn't get involved in his mess in an election year.

His cell phone vibrated in his pocket. He had memorized Callahan's number; it was she. He wanted to take it but was too embarrassed to do so in Marge's presence.

Marge said, "Why are you ignoring the call? Tommy Murdoch, you're blushing! It's a girl, isn't it? Don't deny it. Why not answer?"

He shrugged. "It's not a girl, it's maybe the girl, Marge. I met her the day of the…y' know, the shooting. At Division 4."

"She's a cop? She must really like you, Tommy." She looked at him and read the whole story on his face. She wanted to kiss his cheek or maybe tousle his curly hair. She said, "My advice, honey, don't let her get away. Call her back right now."

Tommy said, "I will. It's just…well, I never met anyone quite like her. She's good looking and smart, n' at, but she's bold as brass. That's what Mom used to call people like her, bold as brass. I'm not sure how to handle her, the way she comes on. Like I feel like I'm wrestling with my arms tied behind my back."

As reluctant as Tommy was to discuss his love life with anyone, at least Marge was no stranger. And he found it easier to talk to a surrogate big sister than to an actual big brother.

"Maybe you should cut her some slack, Tommy. She couldn't be a wallflower and hope to survive in the police department. Those boys would eat her alive. Have you had her out to dinner? Not the diner. I mean, a nice place. Have you brought her flowers?"

"Flowers?!" It had never entered his mind.

"Red roses," Marge said. "A dozen…no two, two dozen of the reddest roses you can buy. You know, there's a flower shop downstairs in the arcade."

He did, he knew that, but the speed at which things were suddenly moving had Tommy's head spinning.

In that state, he headed for the bank of elevators.

CHAPTER 12

By the time the elevator lowered him to the lobby, Tommy's stomach was grumbling. He cursed himself for having turned down the half hoagie Marge had offered him. He could almost taste it now. It was pointless to invite Mayor Caliguiri to lunch—Hizzoner had never accepted Tommy's invitations to dine—so he passed the Mayor by and hustled to his car, this time with the wind strongly at his back. The sky still looked the way it had that morning, like lumpy oatmeal.

He was amazed to get any sort of cell reception in his car two stories below the Public Safety Building, but Callahan's voice sounded clear as a bell. She accepted his invitation to dinner later that evening. Indeed it had to be later, since she was in the middle of an 11 to 6 p.m. shift.

He drove to the Squirrel Hill business district, parked in the lot at the corner of Forbes and Murray Avenues, and had a sub and a diet cola at Uncle Shloima's. You don't just walk out of Uncle Shloima's, you waddle out with your legs bowed around a full stomach. He was determined despite the uncomfortable weather that Bobbi, who he knew was waiting patiently in her crate for his arrival home, would get her usual afternoon stroll around the neighborhood. But first he had two errands to perform; one, to call for a late reservation at Marco Vesuvio's Ristorante in Highland Park; and two, to stop at the florist around the corner on Murray to buy two dozen red roses.

*   *   *

Bobbi was happy to hear his footsteps on the stairs, to hear him open the door, to see her guy home at last. She seemed even happier to see the bouquet of long stem red roses he was carrying, thinking they were for her. When she was led to understand they were not for her, Bobbi began to pout. Tommy apologized and told her they were for Callahan, and Bobbi stopped pouting—she approved of Callahan.

Tommy put the flowers in the fridge and was hit with an ugly thought—Willams was in the fridge at the Morgue.

He found his foul weather cap, a fleece-lined one with ear flaps, on the shelf atop his coat closet, and he wrapped a scarf around his neck. He helped Bobbi into her favorite black vinyl jacket, the one that made her look as tough as a biker, and they were off. Tommy was grateful to find the wind had died down to nothing; glad, too, that the lumpy sky was fulfilling its promise. There were snow flurries in the air. Bobbi leaped at them and yapped when a flake settled on the tip of her nose. Tommy laughed at her antics, and until they approached the spot on Plainfield Street where...you know, until then his mind was totally occupied with the upcoming dinner date with Callahan. He wondered if he would ever be able to pass that spot without reliving the...you know.

Having spent a good deal of the day waiting in her crate, Bobbi was a ball of energy. Tommy did his best to keep up with her, but afternoon naps are addictive and he was looking forward to one.

CHAPTER 13

Arthur and Nina had an engagement that evening, some sort of charity event, so the BMW was occupied. Tommy had to make do with the Dart. Luckily he found a parking spot for it right outside Callahan's building.

She invited him in and was so pleased to see the flowers in his arms. She thanked him with a hug and a smooch on the cheek. She had no vase big enough for two dozen roses, but she made do with an aluminum pitcher she used to make ice tea. She set the roses in its makeshift vase on the little table by the settee. They stood for a minute admiring the effect, she clutching his arm to her.

Callahan was wearing dark brown slacks, matching silk top and ankle-high suede boots. An amulet of green stone that looked Native American hung to her cleavage by a leather thong. With her malted milk skin and hair as dark as midnight, he thought her alluring and exotic. Tommy was smitten. His hands shook as he helped her on with her coat.

* * *

They had a way to go, traveling east through the North Side, roughly parallel to the Allegheny River. As they crossed the river via the Highland Park Bridge, they shared a laugh.

She said, "You're serious? Bobbi really thought the roses were for her? Aw, now I feel bad for her."

"She got over it when I explained they were for you. She likes you a lot, Callahan."

"I have an idea. Bring her over to my place, either tomorrow or Sunday. Will you do that, please, Tommy? I'll share the roses with her. Poor dear, she loves you so much. Will you, please?"

Tommy said he would. If only he weren't driving, he wanted so badly to hug her.

*　*　*

As they reached the east bank of the river and approached Highland Park, Callahan said, "Isn't the entrance to the Zoo just ahead?"

"We're approaching the back entrance to the Park, but yes, the main entrance of the Zoo is right around the next bend. We'll be passing the City's reservoir system soon, too."

"I'm pretty familiar with this area, Tommy. I haven't been around here for a couple of years, but this is part of Division 6, and Division 6 was my first assignment in the cops." She let that float for a few beats. "For a very short time. You might as well know, I had a little trouble with my C.O."

"Oh?"

"He got a little too familiar, what my dad used to call taking liberties. Busy hands, Tommy. Too busy for my taste." She shrugged. "I had to teach him some manners. I did, I dealt with it, but I also got transferred out of Division 6."

"You dealt with it."

"I did. Believe me, I paid close attention in those hand-to-hand combat classes at the Academy. Some time I'll show you a few of my favorite moves."

"Promise?"

Callahan hugged his arm. "Promise."

She does that a lot, Tommy thought, *hugs my arm. Jeez.*

*   *   *

The Dart wound its way from the Allegheny River toward the top of the eastern bluff. It worked its way up by hilly, narrow streets on the edge of Highland Park, and just as it was about to reach the City's reservoir system Tommy took it right and right again—two turns and there was Bryant Street. Two blocks down Bryant was the once single-family residence of white brick that had been converted to Marco Vesuvio's Ristorante. Its once wooden porch had long ago been removed and its once small front yard was paved over for patio dining under the stars, from May through the middle of September.

As he pulled into the parking lot across the street, Tommy said, "Don't be embarrassed if they make a fuss over us. Chef Marco was a high school buddy of Artie's, they're really good friends. We know his whole family and they know ours. We eat here a lot."

"I didn't even know it was here," Callahan said. "Just as well, I guess. I probably couldn't have afforded it on a rookie cop's salary."

Indeed a fuss was made when they entered the restaurant. Two Mrs. Vesuvios, Chef Marco's wife, Tina, and his mother, who Tommy called Mama V, were greeting patrons, as they usually did, as they entered the front door. Mama V pinched Tommy's cheek, also as usual. A larger fuss was made over Callahan because Tommy had never ever shown up at Vesuvio's with a girl on his arm. Except for a few years ago, the ladies recalled, when Tommy would show up with his mother.

"It smells amazing in here," Callahan said.

After the cheek pinching, the elder Mrs. Vesuvio took Tommy aside and whispered, "Am I right thinking this is serious between you and this sweet girl, Thomas?" She nodded, her eyebrows danced.

"I hope so, Mama V," he replied. "I sure do hope so."

Mama Vesuvio passed the honor of showing the couple to their table to her daughter-in-law, since she was not fond of climbing stairs and Tommy had requested a table in the quieter dining area on the second floor.

*   *   *

After first courses of Caesar salad with anchovies, they were enjoying glasses of Chianti Classico, complimentary sides of pasta and later, their entrees. Callahan said, "You were right about Chef Marco's meatballs. I taste three different meats and at least one kind of cheese in this one. How's your veal?"

"Hm? Fine, my veal is fine. Chef Marco will be out to say hello sooner or later. You can ask for his meatball recipe."

"Oh, he wouldn't..." Her date was enjoying his meal well enough, Callahan saw, but still Tommy seemed preoccupied, staring at her then off into space, frowning, lost in thought. "What's wrong, Tommy? Do I have marinara on my face? You stare at me then you go a million miles away. Something's troubling you. The shooting, I guess. Not that I blame you, honey, but..."

But it wasn't worry over the shooting or the upcoming hearing that had Tommy in a funk. It was something else, something that Marge had said earlier that afternoon that troubled him now, and the same thing, while unstated, was implied in Mama Vesuvio's winks and nods.

He said, "I'm thinking about me, what I can and can't do. I'm smart enough about some things: taking care of myself and Bobbi, getting around the City doing my job. I'm a good investigator, Callahan, I really am. I'm effective. Even Artie admits that I am. But by now you must have caught on to the fact that some things, social things, I just don't seem to get. So okay, that's where I am, I don't get it. Everybody wants to know, are we as serious about each other as we appear to be? How do they know? Do we appear to be serious? I don't get it. And they say, I better not let you get away."

"Oh, I'm sure they don't mean anything by it, Tommy. I'm sure they mean well."

"Like Mom used to say, That's all well and good. That is, unless you consider this: How do I stop you from getting away, if you decide to get away? I don't have a clue. Like I said, there are things I just don't get."

Callahan put down her fork and was about to reply when, as Tommy had predicted, Chef Marco made his appearance. Attired from head to foot in white poplin shirt and trousers and wrapped in a huge white apron with only a few stains of marinara sauce. Perched on the head of the little round man was a high white chef's toque. He stood only an inch or two over five feet, and by the size of his belly, Marco appeared to be his own biggest fan. He opened his arms to Tommy, who stood and was pulled into a bear hug against that great belly. Then Marco reached into a pocket of his apron and pulled out a little baggie.

He said, "A meatball for Bobbi. Her favorite, with red clam sauce."

Marco asked after the health of Artie, Nina and the kids before turning his attention to Callahan. He said, "And this is the beautiful lady with no first name. Callahan, is it?"

"It's Elizabeth," Callahan said. She was surprised how quickly news traveled from the front door back to the kitchen. She complimented the chef on his delicious food and the lovely facility the restaurant was. He took her hand, bowed over it in a continental way.

He said, "It's a pleasure to cook for such a lovely lady. You'll honor us many times, I hope, Elizabeth Callahan. You can bring him along, if you wish," he said, nodding at Tommy.

He was needed back in the kitchen. He waddled off in that direction, waving to patrons, stopping for a word here and there.

"You heard that, the way he said it?" Tommy asked. "Elizabeth Callahan. Everybody thinks we're serious or knows we are, and they're depending on me to stop you from getting away. Do I know how to do that? No, I do not."

Callahan was happy to have met Chef Marco, happy too for the intrusion, which gave her time to sort out her feelings and come up with the right words to explain things to Tommy.

She said, "I'd never suggest that you ignore what your friends tell you. That wouldn't be right because I know they mean well. They're happy for you, they obviously want the best for you. If they think I represent the best for you, then good for them. Don't ignore them, try to understand what it is they're doing. They're showing you that they care.

"But when it comes to keeping me around, I'm the only reliable source. Come and ask me." She tapped herself on the chest.

"We're not kids anymore, Tommy, you and me. No doubt, my biological clock is ticking. I've ignored it so far, but the ticking is getting louder, harder to ignore. Still, I'm in no hurry. Get married, raise a family? Sure, some day. But before I settle down I'd like to enjoy a courtship. I'd like to be able to take my time and enjoy having a guy seriously in love with me. You get what I mean? I don't think that's asking too much, do you?"

He wasn't sure which reply was the correct one, yes or no.

"Oh, Tommy, no, please don't frown. I'm saying, it's early days but I think that guy is you. I hope it is. Understand?"

He brightened, thinking that maybe he had succeeded, without knowing how, in not letting her get away. He wasn't positive, but he nodded anyway.

*　*　*

Tommy pulled up outside Callahan's building and they kissed before leaving the car. He saw her to her door, where they kissed again. She said, "Come on in for a while."

"Are you gonna show me some of your favorite moves?"

"Not tonight. But I'll show you the one I usually show my dates."

"Which is…"

"The one where I throw you down the fire escape."

CHAPTER 14

Saturday morning.

The door of Bobbi's wire crate was never actually locked, so she was able to exit the crate when she recognized Arthur's tread on the stairs. The door to Tommy's apartment was never locked, either, so when Arthur walked into the bedroom, Bobbi joined him in front of her master. Tommy was sitting on the edge of his bed, not yet fully awake.

"Talk about your morning after," Artie said. "What happened to you last night? You look like you were wrestling with a bear." Instead of answering, Tommy looked up at his big brother with a Cheshire grin on his face. Artie groaned. He said, "Oh no, not again."

"Yeah, Artie, I'm in love, and it's real this time."

"It was real all the other times, too. Except it wasn't."

It had been real so many times, Artie had come to believe his little brother fell in love with every woman he ever met. But time and again Tommy had misread the women's signals, misunderstood their intentions, and time and again the romances ended in disappointment.

Artie directed his next remark to the only other person in the room with any sense. He said, "Bobbi, it's about time we pounded some sense into this guy, don't you think?"

The dog was standing with her front paws on Tommy's knees. She turned to look up at Artie and arf-ed at him. That led Artie to pause, for he, like the rest of the family, had come to trust Bobbi's instincts.

Artie sat on the bed, arm over his brother's shoulder and hugged Tommy to him. He said, "You better start from the beginning and tell me everything." He glanced at his wristwatch. "I've got a brunch to attend in an hour, so make it the short version."

Tommy said, "We're not going to the IHOP?"

It was not a ritual, at least not one set in stone, but the two brothers would often go to the IHOP for breakfast on Saturday mornings. Their lives were too complicated for them to manage it every single one, just most of them. Tommy was disappointed that it was not on for this morning.

"That's what I came up to tell you, I've got a conflict this morning. Actually it's a conflict I created myself. I arranged a brunch meeting and invited all the players involved in Monday's hearing: the Police Commissioner and Chief Barancovich of Internal Affairs, Grossman from the Post-Gazette, what's her name, Pritz, from the Trib, Leroy Evans of the New Courier. Bender of KDKA TV, too. I'm not sure they'll all show up, but I know for sure I've got a rabbi, two priests and one Baptist minister coming, in addition to Reverend Paine." He thought over what he had said and decided that most of his invitees wouldn't pass up free eats. "I think they'll all show. The Rev will definitely be there. He's the biggest appetite in town. I'm only kidding, you know? He's a friend of mine."

This news really distressed Tommy.

He said, "Why news people? Why all the clergy? The Rev? Jeez, Artie, you're making a big tzimis out of this." The brothers often heard words that used to come out of their mother's mouth coming unintentionally out of theirs.

"Listen, bro. Reverend Duvall Paine is one of the most influential people, if not the most influential person in the black community. Believe me, we need to involve him and we need the support of the media people, too. Besides, I hate to say this, but you're the one who made a tzimis, not me. A white detective shooting and killing a black man on a quiet street in one of Pittsburgh's wealthiest neighborhoods? You don't think that's making a tzimis? I'm just doing what I can to put a lid on the pot.

"Now, no more talk about that. Before I have to run, tell me about this girl you're in love with."

So Tommy swallowed the lump of anger that had stuck in his throat. He told his brother everything, or almost everything, starting with his meeting Callahan on the stairs of Division 4 and ending with their dining at Vesuvio's the previous night. Since his relationship with Callahan was only a week old, the short version and the long one were the same.

Artie said, "So it's Callahan? No first name?"

"Of course she has a first name, Elizabeth, but she likes me to call her just plain Callahan, so I do."

Artie looked at the beagle. "And you approve, Bobbi? Well, that's a first. I'll tell you what. When you see her, invite her to Sunday brunch here at our house. I'll tell Nina she's coming. The girls will be thrilled to meet Uncle Tommy's newest sweetheart."

"I don't know, Artie," Tommy said. "She might have to report for duty on Sunday."

"In that case," Artie said as he stood to leave, "she can tell her C.O. she was called before the District Attorney. And tell her she can come in uniform. The girls will get a huge kick out of that."

CHAPTER 15

The weatherman had promised the sun would make an appearance later that Saturday afternoon, but it was approaching noon and so far, no show. Looking out of her window at the sky, Callahan shook her head. She saw nothing but gray, and she was willing to swear it tasted as if snow were in the air.

Her guests, Tommy and Bobbi, were due to arrive at noon. Her two-seater dining table was set informally as if for a picnic, with paper ware left over from Halloween. Sandwiches had been constructed, sandwiches that Callahan considered her specialty—thick slices of ham with two kinds of cheese and a thin slice of tomato, all stacked on an Italian roll. They were in the fridge ready to be popped into the toaster oven.

She had wrapped a pillow with an old beach towel and placed it on the floor near the table. Using a paring knife, she had skimmed the thorns off the long stems of two blood red roses. She placed the two roses on the pillow for Bobbi, hoping this would seal their friendship. The remaining roses in their aluminum pitcher occupied the place of honor in the center of the table. The roses were not yet threatening to wilt, but now and then a petal would drop. Callahan refused to consider that an ill omen

In the bedroom, she checked herself in the mirror mounted above her dresser. Hair, okay. She was glad she had washed out the dash of pink dye before last night's dinner date; she thought Tommy liked her hair better without it. She had chosen to wear jeans and a gold pullover sweater, a very casual look except that Callahan's chest did things to a sweater that even the manufacturer hadn't counted on. She wanted to look hot, but calmly hot, because she wanted Tommy to feel comfortable with her, especially comfortable with her today in her apartment. She knew she ought to slow their romance down, but dear Lord, she ached for him. She stepped into simple black flats and went to answer the door.

* * *

While Tommy and Callahan were taking their time saying hello, Bobbi investigated every inch of the apartment, wagging and sniffing, wagging and sniffing. It took her no time at all to understand the intention of the pillow with two roses. She sauntered over to Callahan and offered her a paw, this time not to shake but to just hold for a moment. It was a significant moment for them both; a breathless moment for Callahan. She discovered what Tommy already knew: to peer deeply into the eyes of a beagle was to change your heart forever.

Callahan popped the sandwiches into the toaster oven and poured their drinks. Bobbi settled down on the pillow when her master and her new dear friend took their seats at the table.

They ate and talked. Tommy passed on Artie's invitation for Callahan to join the family for Sunday brunch. Callahan stopped chewing.

She said, "So they want to meet me tomorrow morning?!" It was both a question and a statement loaded with apprehension. Callahan swallowed whole the bite she had taken and put down the rest of her sandwich. Suddenly her appetite had fled. "Oh, Tommy, they won't like me, I know they won't. They're such…you know," she said with a hand gesture, "they're such important people and I'm…"

"Don't I know who you are, Callahan? Look, they're not what you think, they're really nice people. Artie… What can I say about my brother?" Tommy scratched behind his right ear. "Sure, Artie is the D.A., but even when he wasn't the D.A. or a hotshot prosecutor, when he was only my brother, he was really a…" He couldn't quite bring himself to say, nice guy, he wasn't used to admitting his bossy big brother was actually a nice guy. "He's really…all right. And Nina, his wife, is beautiful and smart, and the girls, well, I just love them to pieces.

"Really, Callahan, they're wonderful people. Their only fault, and I'm sure other people wouldn't consider it a fault, they're too damn protective of me. Is that a fault? Yeah, well, I don't know."

"I don't think it's a fault," Callahan said. "Y'know, it's my job as a police officer, protecting people, and I love doing my job. It's been a while since I've had a family protecting me. The idea sounds kinda nice."

Tommy shook his head. Bobbi, sleeping among bent green stems and mutilated rose petals, yipped at a rabbit she was chasing in her dream.

Tommy said, "But they're not looking for another person to protect, they're looking for someone other than themselves to take over protecting me. That's what they'll want to hear you say, that you love being a cop because it gives you the opportunity to protect people. They'll think you're a person they can trust to look out for me. Oh, they're gonna love you, Callahan."

He looked down at his plate, his cheeks highly colored with embarrassment. "I've always been the little brother that needed to be looked after. In their minds I still am. I'm pretty sure Mom made Artie promise to look after me. He doesn't know that I know, but I know. And he has looked after me, he's never stopped looking after me. And Nina does, too, and even the girls do. So when they see they can give over to you, they'll love you, Callahan. Believe me, they will."

* * *

While Tommy, Bobbi and Callahan were lunching at her apartment, something was going down on Grant Street—unusual for a Saturday morning. There was activity at Roscoe's Luncheonette.

Strangers to downtown Pittsburgh could walk along Grant on the other side of the street from the City-County Building, and even if their stride was leisurely, the strangers were not likely to notice they had strolled past Roscoe's, it was that tiny a place with that narrow a front. Imagine it as the club car of a passenger train, if you are of an age to remember club cars and passenger trains.

The proprietor of Roscoe's was not named Roscoe, it was a Vietnamese immigrant by the name of Ernie Tran. Ernie claimed to have purchased Roscoe's from a woman named Wilma...something, Ernie's English was that hard to understand. He wasn't sure from whom Wilma...something had purchased it, but he was sure it was not from anyone named Roscoe. Ernie didn't know if there had ever been a Roscoe at Roscoe's, and he didn't think it mattered.

Customers were not served at Roscoe's, they phoned in their lunch orders to Roscoe's—only sandwiches, soft drinks and two choices of chips, barbeque or nacho—and only on Monday through Friday mornings, and only if they were employed in one of three downtown buildings: the City-County, the Public Safety or the New Federal. Any other buildings were out of walking distance for the many

ₓran children who delivered the orders to the
.omers' desks at noon.

Each weekday morning or during lunchtime or in
the hour immediately following lunchtime, Roscoe's
was a hive of activity and noise. No one would want
to congregate there at that time. However, later in
the afternoon, after the sun had begun to settle into
the west below the confluence of rivers that became
the Ohio, after that time a group could gather and
conspire in peace, quiet and relative secrecy.

There were two 8-seater round tables in Roscoe's—no room for any more, not even a single twofer.
The tables were usually piled high with cardboard
cartons of chips and cans of soda pop. That morning
the cartons had been cleared away to make room
for Ernie Tran's catering efforts, which consisted of
piling onto the tables the sandwiches, bags of chips
and cans of soda that were the usual weekday fare,
only they were displayed on round platters instead
of delivered in shoebox-sized cartons.

Ernie was occupied arranging sandwiches on platters when the host of the meeting, District Attorney
Arthur Murdoch, arrived, followed almost immediately by his invitees: cops, clergy, jurists, journalists,
lawyers and pols; all packing into the tiny, narrow
room like sardines pressed into a tin can. The room
soon reeked of a mix of sweat and expensive af-
ter-shave lotions. There were more people invited
than there were chairs, but the print and visual media

reps were happy to stand, making it easier for them to reach the eats.

Arthur cleared his throat and asked for and got the attention of attendees quickly. He was the District Attorney, after all, an elected official of considerable authority even though it was supposedly a social not an official function. Arthur was, for him, casually dressed in one of his gray pinstripe suits, but with his shirt collar open and no tie.

He leaned against the door to prevent anyone's coming or going, and said, "If the word gets out that this was a fundraiser for my re-election campaign, the Democratic Party's ethics committee is liable to squawk that the meal and the hall I hired were too elaborate and expensive."

That got laughs from everyone but Ernie Tran. Someone piped up, "I didn't know we had an ethics committee."

Arthur replied, "It's not a very active committee. Anyways," he continued, "those of you who know me well know this couldn't be a fundraiser. You are all my good friends, and I never ask my good friends for money."

Jeers and denials at that one.

"If I'm not asking you for money, why did I invite you here this morning? In case you've been out of town and haven't already heard, we have[a hearing scheduled for Monday morning concerning, as you well know, the shooting of an African-American male in the City's Squirrel Hill neighborhood. And there's absolutely no doubt we've had all the shootings of black males by white law enforcement officers that we can stand."

He didn't expect to get any objections to that, and he got none.

"Black lives matter, yes they do indeed, and we've instituted programs that we're confident will make all the difference in easing tensions between the races in our community. I don't need to tell you any of this, you already know it."

They did, they all knew about the new programs, although some were more skeptical than others about the outcomes.

"This time," Arthur continued, "of which you're also aware, the shooter happens to be my brother, Thomas, who clearly had no choice in the matter and who did exactly what we'd all have done if we were in the same situation as Tommy found himself."

Arthur paused, looked individually at their faces for confirmation. He mostly got it.

"I'm asking a favor from you all. The favor is this, that we follow procedure to the letter for the hearing, as usual. That we do it by the book, but..." He raised an open hand and wiggled it. "...but without turning Monday's hearing into a kangaroo court, and without pointless demonstrations of protest that will accomplish nothing but to embarrass me, and maybe destroy my little brother."

"Arthur?" A distinguished-looking, middle-aged man stood up. He had a shock of white hair in a dated pompadour style, and he was dressed in ministerial black. Father C.T. Belleau was well known to the invitees as a Pittsburgher born-and-raised. He was the principal of Central Catholic High School, and an outspoken liberal.

"You have something, C.T.?" Arthur asked.

"I do. Seems to me if we don't soft pedal this shooting, we'll be aiming the national spotlight on Pittsburgh as a violent town, like Chicago or Detroit. That our streets aren't safe. Wasn't the shooting at the Tree of Life Synagogue enough bad publicity for Pittsburgh?"

The city editor of the Post-Gazette, Bernard Grossman, was on his feet. He said, "You're not asking us to look the other way, as if the shooting never happened?"

"I would never ask you to do that, Bernie," Arthur said. "I'm only asking that we not make a mountain out of a molehill, here."

Evans from the New Courier was on his feet, too. He was about to add something to the mix, but he stopped with his mouth agape, as he noticed that Reverend Duvall Paine, seated at one of the round tables, had begun the process of standing. Being nearly seven feet tall and nearly eighty years of age, he took his time doing so. Actually, he unwound rather than stood, all the while pressing one of his huge hands against a crick that was plaguing his lower back.

He said, "Excuse my interruption, Brother Leroy, but I would like to voice some agreement with my colleague, Father Belleau." He turned in the priest's direction. "C.T., I believe your point is right on about what that kind of publicity would do to our fair city. Furthermore, I call to everyone's attention the fact that this man, this black man, Willams, was a violent criminal. I'd rather not have the nation talking about violent black men. There's been enough talk connecting black men and violence, we don't need any more."

The tiny room echoed with expressions of agreement with the Rev and Father Belleau.

Seeing that he had accomplished his mission, Arthur suggested they dig in to the food before Ernie Tran decided to slop it to the hogs.

* * *

Later that same Saturday afternoon, Tommy and Callahan watched an old movie they had both seen before but decided they wanted to enjoy together. Later they called for pizza delivery, and when the pizza was gone and Bobbi had been fed and walked around Callahan's neighborhood, they chose another movie to watch that they knew was deserving of more attention than it was likely to get. In the trunk of his Dart Tommy had stashed a gym bag in which he had packed a toothbrush, a comb and a change of underwear in case he had, for a change, correctly interpreted signals he had picked up from Callahan. Just when he thought his prospects were looking up, Callahan suddenly took a breath and stood up from the settee.

She said, "Tommy, dear, we've only known each other for five days. I think things are moving too fast."

"Actually," he replied, "It's only been 4 ½ days. You're counting Tuesday as one day, but we didn't meet until the middle of Tuesday afternoon."

She shook her head and laughed. "Tommy, Tommy. I'm gonna use the john and get myself back together. You do the same. Okay?"

Tommy sighed. "Okay."

Chapter 16

Arthur didn't seem to grasp the meaning of the word casual when it came to clothing. Tommy thought his brother probably even played golf in a gray pinstripe suit. At this moment at the head of the family dining table at Sunday brunch, Arthur was dressed, as usual, in one his many gray pinstripe suits. In his hand was a sandwich of lox, bagel and cream cheese.

He called out over laughter and chatter, "Can someone please explain to Ms. Callahan and the rest of us, too, why my two beautiful daughters are dressed identically this morning? Please?"

Nina was in the middle of explaining that very thing to Callahan, so she raised her voice to include everyone else. The two girls—Edie, eleven and Madison, nine, both blue-eyed blond clones of their mother—were dressed identically in white pinafores, black Mary Jane shoes and identical pink ribbons in their hair. Callahan thought that if she were to have a sister—which she unfortunately never had—she just knew they would not want to dress alike, they would want to assert their independence from each other.

Tommy thought nothing of the way his nieces were dressed, to him they always looked lovely, no matter what they were wearing. But he nodded agreement with his brother, an explanation was due.

"It's their latest schtick," Nina said to Callahan, reaching over to touch the hand of her guest who was sitting to her left. "At home, at school, driving everybody crazy. They're pretending to be twins. They even talk in unison."

"Yes we do," the girls chimed in, as one.

The women and girls laughed.

Nina said. "Yesterday they told me they remember being nursed at the same time, one on each breast."

The men grimaced, but again the women laughed.

The girls were encouraged by the women's reactions. They were wriggling in chairs to Nina's right, across from their Uncle and their guest. They put their heads together and whispered to each other. A decision was reached. Edie, the older of the two, asked Callahan if she had fallen in love with Uncle Tommy at first sight? And Madison wanted to know if she intended to marry him.

Nina apologized for her daughters' impertinence. They were so precocious, Nina thought she was inured to being stunned by what came out of them. She was wrong.

It had been a waste of time, Callahan realized, to have worried that her being in uniform would intimidate the girls. Those questions were whoppers. She decided the only way to deal with those two precocious youngsters was to ignore their ages and speak to them as if they were grown women.

She said, "When I first met your Uncle Tommy, he looked so forlorn, so …so vulnerable, I didn't want to marry him, I wanted to mother him."

That got a laugh from everyone except Tommy.

Callahan was encouraged to go on, but she was interrupted by the ringing of a telephone in the kitchen. The ring was recognized by the family sitting around the table as the must-be-picked-up line from Arthur's office.

Artie excused himself and, although he didn't look happy about being disturbed on Sunday, he went to answer it. When he returned after a few minutes, he dropped a bomb in the middle of the dining room table:

"Tomorrow's hearing has been postponed!"

Captain Barancovich had called, Artie told them, to notify both Murdoch brothers that S.L.P.D. had located Odell Willams's next of kin. Madison, the younger of the two girls, asked her dad what was an S.L.P.D., what was a next of kin and, most importantly, who was Odell Willams?

Nina asked Tommy if it wasn't time for Bobbi's morning walk. He either didn't hear her or didn't catch on, which didn't surprise Nina about her brother-in-law. She looked at Callahan, who gave Tommy an elbow in the ribs.

"Huh? Oh, yeah." He said to his nieces, "Why don't you girls go get Bobbi and walk her around the block? You know how to put on her harness, don't you, Edie?"

Of course she knew how. The girls frowned at each other, knowing full well why they were being dismissed. Grownups. Still, they loved Bobbi.

Before leaving, Madison went around the table to hold a brief, whispered conversation with Callahan. Then Madison, apparently satisfied with what she had been told, followed her sister out of the room. Her parents wanted to know what that was all about.

Callahan said, "Madison wanted to know if they were supposed to call me Aunt Callahan. I told her she could call me Elizabeth or Liz or Betty. Whichever she chose would be alright. But the aunt part was a little premature. She seemed to understand. Smart as a whip, that little one."

Both of them were, they all agreed. Of course, what Tommy wanted to know was, why was the hearing postponed?

Artie had the answer from Captain Barancovich: the Saint Louis, Missouri Police had managed to locate an aunt, Odell Willams's mother's older sister. She claimed to be the last of the Willams family, now that her nephew was gone. She claimed to not have much in the way of funds, but she was coming to Pittsburgh to claim the body. According to Barancovich, the old lady said, 'she wanted to attend the hearing into her nephew's shooting, if only they could see their way clear to holding off till she could get there.'

Barancovich had no choice, according to Artie, who had it from Barancovich himself, no choice but to postpone the hearing until Wednesday at ten a.m.

"Wednesday? Ten a.m. Wednesday?" Tommy stood, losing the napkin from his lap to the floor.

"It takes a while, from St. Louis to Pittsburgh." Artie shrugged. "Especially if you're coming by Greyhound."

Tommy groaned. What in hell was he supposed to do between then and Wednesday? Nina and Artie looked at Callahan.

She said, "I'm sure I can help keep him busy till Wednesday."

* * *

Callahan helped Nina clear the table. While the women were getting better acquainted in the kitchen, Tommy was asking a favor of his brother:

"Could you call Reverend Paine for me? I need an intro. I want an appointment. I've decided I need to talk to him. You did say he was a friend of yours."

"Not an old friend," Artie said, "but, yes, definitely a friend. I first met him when I was running for City Council. I first saw him when I was still in grade school and he was playing basketball for Duquesne University. Dad used to take me to watch him play at Duquesne Gardens, and they played in tournaments on National TV, too."

At present the basketball program at Duquesne was a shadow of its former self, according to Artie. In the late 50's the Dukes of Duquesne University were one of America's greatest teams, and Duvall Paine was its greatest player. In a reminiscing mood, Artie recalled watching Paine make Bill Mlkvy, Temple University's Owl Without a Vowel, look like he had two left feet. Duvall Paine was All-Star quality, slated for stardom in the pros. But instead he got the calling.

"That's right, Tommy. Instead of going into the pros, he went to a seminary somewhere in North Carolina. Gave up the NBA, the fame, the National spotlight, to become a minister. Nobody in town could believe it, there he was one day in the Sports head-lines and the next day he was gone." Artie shrugged.

Paine came back to the 'burgh after graduating from the seminary, returned to his home town to be-come, first, the assistant minister at Ebeneazer Baptist Church in Homewood, and later to found his own congregation, the First Church of the Redeemer, also in Homewood. He and Artie met there when Artie was getting into politics in a serious way.

"Seems like a long time ago, Tommy. Duvall Paine must be at least 80 by now, an old man. He'll be at the hearing Wednesday, I'm sure of that. You're liable to say something to him you shouldn't."

"You always say that about me, Artie."

"And it's always true."

Tommy was slowly but surely working himself into a pout. "Then you won't call him for me?"

"You're not going to make confession to him, are you, like the goyim do?"

"Artie, we are the goyim."

"Only half, only Dad's half. On Mom's half we're not."

"If I promise not to confess like the goyim, will you call him?"

Artie frowned but finally agreed. "You know where his church is, on Homewood Avenue? Catty corner from the Trader Joe's?"

* * *

It was the Sunday afternoon before Thanksgiving; it was the kind of Sunday afternoon that everyone who lived north of the Mason-Dixon Line prayed for but seldom got: a day for sun glasses, a lighter jacket, a cap without earflaps, and November air that might sneak a love nip at your cheek, but wouldn't actually bite.

It was a free Sunday afternoon for Tommy, who was on paid leave until after the hearing; a sort-of free afternoon for Callahan, too, since in order to get the free morning to meet all the Murdochs, she had to take the Third Watch (11 p.m. to 7 a.m.).

The real beneficiary of the free Sunday was the beagle. Tommy and Callahan walked Bobbi all over the Squirrel Hill neighborhood and into Schenley Park. She crunched into every pile of crisp russet leaves, sniffed every trail for squirrel or chipmunk, snorted at every bed of mums. By the look of the mums and pumpkins that people had placed to decorate their porch stoops, night frost had taken its toll; they would soon be nothing but mush. On this Sunday afternoon, though, the mums, the leaves, the pumpkins were doing their best to put on a show.

Anyone following their rather aimless progress through the November Sunday afternoon, strolling along behind the beagle, taking turns holding the leash, holding hands, chatting, learning little intimate things about each other, anyone would have known they were in love.

Later, after being fed her dinner, Bobbi was more than content to snuggle into her crate. Tommy and Callahan found a tiny Middle Eastern café in the Shadyside neighborhood that was mostly empty at the dinner hour. The sense that the place was failing was oppressive, but the hummus was superb and the pita was fresh and hot.

Callahan said, "You're going to see him when, tomorrow in the late morning? I don't agree with

Arthur, I think it's wise to talk to somebody besides me when something is eating at you, Tommy. Talking things over with me, sometimes I'll be able to help, sometimes not."

She paused several beats to separate what she had just said from what she was about to say.

"Everybody has good things to say about Reverend Paine. I've heard he's the real McCoy, a man who loves people and they love him. Not the political leader but the moral leader of the Black Community. Church-goers especially love him.

"But if I were you, dear, in your place, and if I had what you experienced on my mind, I'd want to talk to Sergeant Kenneth McKenzie. Remember him?"

"If you mean that tough old bird from the Police Academy firing range, who could forget him."

She said, "He scared the shit out of this rookie, excuse my French, but he worked on me until I could finally, like, hit the broad side of a barn. If I wasn't too far away."

"I do remember the guy," Tommy said. He did indeed, but the talk of the man and the firing range made Tommy realize he had forgotten about his H&K. He no longer missed the weight of it at the small of his back.

Lately, Callahan told him, she had been chewing over what she remembered that Sergeant McKenzie had said to her and her classmates after they had all qualified to carry firearms:

> *Before you rookies strap that weapons belt around your waist, you outa give some thought to what you might have to do with it.*

That's what Sergeant McKenzie said to Callahan's class of rookies at the Police academy, and she admitted that remembering his words troubled her now. Troubled her because she realized she hadn't done it, she hadn't given careful thought to what she might have to do with her weapon.

She said, "I guess I thought if and when the time came, I would do...well, I would do whatever I had to."

She nodded. "Yeah, if I were you, Tommy, maybe I'd go talk with Sergeant McKenzie."

CHAPTER 17

From somewhere above the Great Lakes, an icy wind blew out of Canada and knifed its way across the U.S. northern border, penetrating deeply into the heart of Pennsylvania with the express purpose of greeting Pittsburghers as they stumbled out of bed on Monday morning. On TV there was talk of a foot of snow in Erie. When Tommy left his carriage apartment that morning, he found the skies were as gray as his brother Artie's suits (without the pinstripes). Leaves that had leapt into the gutters were no longer crisp, and the wind wanted to blow his cap off. Tommy tugged it way down over his ears.

He breakfasted, as was his habit on Mondays, at the diner on Baum Boulevard. While working his way through a Belgian waffle, he decided, since he had time before his appointment with Reverend Paine, to take Callahan's advice and try to see Sergeant Kenneth McKenzie.

Before leaving the diner, Tommy called Saint Al's to inquire about his buddy, Mickey Skruggs.

The gist of the phone conversation:

Was he a relative? If not, they were not authorized to release that information. Not even to a County Detective? Well, that was different. Mr. Skruggs was discharged over the weekend into the care of his brother, Charles A. Skruggs. Did he require the address or phone number? No, he did not. Thank you for the information. Goodbye.

*   *   *

Next he punched in the number he had for Charlie Skruggs. Charlie's wife, Marna, answered:

Michael was asleep at the moment and probably would be for several hours. Best to visit around mealtime, Michael could use some help eating and would appreciate the company. Why not come this   evening at 5? Of course, you'll stay for dinner, Thomas. See you then, bye.

*   *   *

Tommy retrieved his Dart and headed along Baum Boulevard toward the business district of East Liberty. Passing several car dealerships, new and used, he thought it was probably time to trade for a newer vehicle, something nicer to escort Callahan in. One of those small Japanese SUVs, maybe. Maybe take her along to pick it out. He thought she would like that; he knew he would.

He drove past the old bank building that had recently been converted to condos and past the Home Depot. At the high school he hung a right and rode Negley Run Boulevard to the Police & Fire Academy. As he turned onto Washington Boulevard and into the Academy parking lot, he noticed he had a stranglehold on the steering wheel. He really had no desire to become re-acquainted with Sergeant Kenneth McKenzie. Tommy remembered him as a massive man, well over six feet four or five, hulking shoulders and a neck as wide as his head. He also remembered angry, deep-set eyes under a Neanderthal's ridge of bony forehead. All in all he thought McKenzie was a hard drinking knuckle dragger, but he knew he could count on McKenzie to know everything there was to know about guns and other lethal weapons. With the aura of a killer about him, just about everybody feared McKenzie, not only the rookies but his superior officers as well.

* * *

The Allegheny River was within a few hundred yards of the Academy. With the wind blowing from the south across the river, Tommy could smell its slightly rancid odor as he left his car. The lot had few vehicles. He expected the building to be deserted as well, with the prolonged holiday season approaching. The next rookie class would not begin training until after the start of the new year.   Tommy's unhurried footsteps echoed in the empty hallway as he approached the firing range office. He looked in through the open door. It was a tiny crowded space with battered, wooden cast-off furniture. Finding the office unoccupied, Tommy turned away, relieved.

"You looking for me, son," someone called.

Tommy saw the man coming up the hall toward him. It was Sergeant McKenzie, no doubt, but an altered McKenzie, not as imposing or as menacing as the one Tommy remembered from his time at the Academy. In those six years McKenzie's massive body had shrunk a few inches both in height and width, his ramrod posture was now less rigid, his once-hulking shoulders had rounded and sagged forward a bit, and when he drew close enough for Tommy to see McKenzie's eyes, they seemed to have lost the intensity of their laser-like stare.

"I know you, don't I?" McKenzie said. "You was through here a while ago. Maybe three, four years?"

"Six, actually," Tommy said. Tommy introduced himself and told McKenzie that his girl friend, Elizabeth Callahan, suggested he come talk to her old gunnery sergeant.

McKenzie scratched his bald head, then a light came on. "Cute little fireplug of a girl, Prince Valiant haircut, bright eyes? That the one? Yeah, I remember her. She told you to come talk to me? What about?"

Tommy asked him if he had heard about the incident where a man was shot and killed on the street near Division 4?

McKenzie said, "That wasn't you, was it? The shooter? Oh. Say, let's go sit down in my office. It ain't very comfortable but it's the best I got."

When they were seated across from each other in the tiny office, they were practically nose to nose. Each man sat on his side of a tiny wooden desk that would have better suited third graders, size-wise. How embarrassed Tommy would have been if anyone happened by and managed to get a load of this scene. It reminded him of his Mom reading to him from Alice Through the Looking Glass.

McKenzie said, "Now, what's the problem that Callahan girl thinks I can help with? Don't be embarrassed. Out with it."

"Not a problem, exactly, Sergeant," Tommy said. Maybe McKenzie was not the brute Tommy remembered from his days at the Academy, but still Tommy was having trouble getting the words out. He never dreamed he would be talking about feelings, not with McKenzie, not with any man. This was not exactly man talk.

He said, "I don't know, I…" Tommy found it easier to speak if he avoided McKenzie's eyes. Those deep-set, hooded eyes put him off as if he were face to face with a reptile. Better to speak to the brass buttons on McKenzie's uniform shirt.

He said, "I feel like shit, sir. Everybody thinks the perp was worthless, he was a felon, that he deserved what he got. The world's a better place without that bum, that's what people are telling me. It's okay that I killed him, what choice did I have? But how can any of that be true, when every time I think of what I did, I think…"

McKenzie interrupted him.

He said, "If only I could take that back. Would I want that death on my conscience, if I had it to do over again? That what you're saying to yourself, son?"

"Yeah." Tommy nodded and nodded. "Yeah."

McKenzie rested his ham of a hand on Tommy's shoulder. "You don't have to say anything more. I know what it feels like. I been where you are. I know it ain't a good place."

They stayed that way for a while, avoiding each other's eyes, the older man's hand on the younger man's shoulder. No father-son type thing was destined to happen, though; neither man was inclined to talk about feelings. When Tommy realized this, he got up to leave.

McKenzie said, "Mind a little advice from an old dog?"

Tommy turned to face him.

"I take it you and that Callahan girl are an item? Well, here's my advice: Get her out of the cops. Get her out and do it quick, before she gets hurt."

Tommy was caught off guard—his mouth fell open.

"She ain't like you and me, son, she won't pull

the trigger. Her life'll be on the line and she won't shoot. Take it from the guy that trained her. She loves being a cop, she's that kinda girl, but she don't have it in her to shoot. She ain't a killer. Her life'll be on the line and…" McKenzie shook his head.

"She's gonna get herself hurt. I was you, I'd marry her, get her pregnant and keep her pregnant. Get her and keep her off the cops. None a my business, of course, but that's what I'd do, I was you."

Chapter 18

Still parked in the Police Academy lot, Tommy sat behind the wheel of the Dart struggling to get his head together. What had he hoped to accomplish by speaking with Sergeant McKenzie? How did that work out! He did the math. He had gone in to see McKenzie with one problem and came out with two. No, he actually had two problems going in, no sense not counting the one he hoped to discuss with Reverend Paine. So he had two problems going in and came out with three.

Once when he was a teenager, after a troubling incident the details of which now escaped him, Tommy remembered his father telling him:

*   *   *

"Everything that happens in life presents an opportunity to learn something worthwhile. The wise man is one who hunts and hunts until he finds it."

*   *   *

So that was what Tommy was doing, hunting for something worthwhile.

He hadn't learned a thing from McKenzie. Well now, wait a minute. Maybe he had actually learned more than one thing, not necessarily from anything McKenzie said but from what had been palpable in his very presence: that somehow nasty things are survivable. This must be so because McKenzie had survived them. Then there was the other thing, the one thing Tommy hadn't bargained for: no matter how much training one had or how good the training, some people could and would pull the trigger and some people couldn't and wouldn't.

* * *

Tommy started the Dart, thinking it a good thing the Homewood neighborhood was close by, for now he would have to hustle to be on time for his appointment with Reverend Paine. He headed out of the lot with McKenzie's words, Get her out of the cops, ricocheting around in his brain.

* * *

Tommy had phone calls to make, and feeling pressed for time, he violated his own rule and made the calls while cruising at 40 mph along Washington Boulevard. The first call, to his sister-in-law Nina, went to her voice mail: Would she ask Edie and Madison to do their Uncle Tommy a big favor and see to

Bobbi's dinner while he visited with his sick friend, Mickey Skruggs, and his family. The second call was to Callahan, who was doing Second Watch (3 p.m. to 11) at Division 4. She was glad to hear that Tommy was going to spend some quality time with his friend for she knew how worried Tommy was about him. She invited him to drop by at her place on his way home from the Skruggs house.

She said, "I'll have dessert waiting for you."

He thought of Callahan's face, the grin, the gleam in her eyes, when she was saying something sexually suggestive like, she'd have dessert waiting—his groin tingled.

* * *

Tommy had become an expert at predicting the time of day or night by the amount of traffic he encountered on the streets of Pittsburgh except, of course, the narrow, crowded, non-gridded jumble of streets of downtown which were always jammed with vehicles. Also excepting every street in every town in western Pennsylvania which would be eerily deserted during a TV broadcast of a Steelers football game. Since traffic was light as he skirted the edge of East Liberty and stayed light as he eased warily through Homewood, Tommy guessed it was half past three, or so.

* * *

There were a number of sections of the Home-wood neighborhood, some two or three blocks long that Tommy passed, where the streets were free of debris and derelict cars, and where the houses were well maintained. They were inexpensively sided with old-fashioned clapboard or asbestos shingles, but still he could tell they were pridefully maintained by pride-ful people. As he drove deeper into the Homewood neighborhood, however, the pride began to dwindle. The gutters and sidewalks became littered with fast food trash, plastic empties heaved from passing car windows, and there were neglected or abandoned buildings everywhere. Many young men loitered on the street corners. Tommy felt their eyes on him as he drove passed. He hated that feeling, hated that his beloved home town was still a black and white world. Either you were or you weren't. He hated it, but he had to admit that once again he missed the feel of the H&K at his back.

* * *

Apprehension aside, Tommy was looking forward to shaking the hand of Reverend Duvall Paine. Tommy had seen him on TV at the forefront of protest march-es, demanding employment for minority contractors, calling for a fair percentage of low income housing, and, the main source of Tommy's apprehension, he had seen the Rev leading an angry crowd in a chant of Black Lives Matter.

Almost as important to Tommy, he had grown up hearing his big brother talking in awed tones about watching Duvall Paine playing college basketball. Artie had been allowed to accompany their dad to the Duquesne campus to watch as Duvall Paine led the Dukes varsity basketball team to victory. Tommy, at that time, was a mere twinkle in their dad's eye, but he remembered hearing that Duvall Paine was so damn tall and so damn strong and so damn fast and so damn accurate: a legend, although now a mostly-forgotten legend in a Pittsburgh replete with sports legends. Most of those legends were black, come to think of it, and Tommy thought perhaps Black Pittsburgh had better memories than White Pittsburgh did.

* * *

The First Church of the Redeemer, speaking of the building itself, was neither a reflection of Reverend Paine's popularity in the community, which was considerable, nor did it project an image of a successful ministry, which Tommy had heard it was. The building at one time had been a large, independent supermarket that had gone belly up, and to Tommy's eye it still looked abandoned. The sign at the front of the property was the type that, instead of identifying the place as a church, ought to be touting the fact that—today only—one could get—BOGO—two cans of soup for the price of one.

Tommy pulled into the vast parking lot that surrounded the building. He found only one other car there, a Ford sedan that looked even more tired than his Dodge Dart. On the flat roof of the building was a huge cross fashioned from weathered 2 x 4s. The cross swayed in the wind, and looked like the mast of a derelict ship. If this was the First Church of the Redeemer, Tommy wondered what the Second looked like.

As soon as he stepped out of the car, Tommy heard—pong pong pong—the unmistakable sound of a dribbling basketball. He followed the sound around to the back of the building, where he found a half-court basketball setup paved in rough concrete, A net-less hoop and wooden backboard were bolted to the building's rear wall. A huge man was dribbling, sinking jump shots from ten and twelve feet out, dribbling, slam dunking, shot after shot unerringly passing through that metal hoop. An old man, the tallest old man Tommy had ever seen, all 7 feet of him. With such grace, he moved through the air like young smoke. No doubt, Duvall Paine.

The Rev was wearing the bottoms of a gray sweat suit, but instead of the top of the sweat suit, he wore a black sleeveless shirt with a minister's white dog collar. His body was so huge, his head looked disproportionately small; it was shaved clean of hair except for white tufts above the ears. His arms looked too long, his legs looked too long, his feet in ordinary black street shoes looked too long. But he moved with amazing grace.

Tommy figured the Rev had to be at least eighty, but he was still agile, still powerful—a David chiseled out of black marble.

In the middle of the move that should have developed into one of his graceful hook shots, Reverend Paine noticed Tommy standing there and stopped. He ducked into a semi-crouch with both hands on the ball, a standard basketball move Tommy remembered from his tryout with the CCAC team. He knew exactly what it was that The Rev meant for him to do—he sprinted toward the basket. At just the right moment the Rev snapped the ball in Tommy's direction, timed perfectly. It was right there when Tommy leapt toward the hoop and laid it up. The ball hit the bottom of the hoop, rebounded and ricocheted off Tommy's head.

An amused Reverend Paine shook his head, but waited to speak. Then, "You hurt?"

"My pride." Tommy said, "That was one of my classic moves. You're lucky, you don't get to see moves like that every day."

He smiled. "Amen to that."

"I was never any good. I've heard so many stories about your playing days with the Dukes. From my brother. You weren't just good, you were great. They all said the NBA was your destiny."

He shook his head. "They were all wrong, I was destined for here. You're Art Murdoch's brother?"

Tommy introduced himself. He wondered when

he shook that giant's paw whether he'd ever see his own hand again.

"I'm told you want to speak to me." The Rev stood looking down at Tommy with the basketball tucked casually under his arm. "Well, go right on ahead. I'm all ears."

Tommy tried to, but didn't know where to begin.

The Rev prompted him, "Your brother told me you love basketball but can't play worth a lick. Here, give it another try." He passed the ball to Tommy once again, but Tommy just stood there and stared at it. When it became apparent that he wasn't going to shoot, the Rev reassessed the situation and said, "Let's go in where we can sit down. This looks to be a sit down kinda thing."

* * *

He led the way into his private sanctum with Tommy trailing along behind him. It was a tiny space, no more than 10x14 or so, the walls covered with inexpensive paneling and a threadbare throw rug over a floor of unvarnished hardwood. What little furniture there was looked as if it had come from Goodwill, but when Tommy sank into a huge, throne-like wing chair across from the Rev, he felt almost hugged by it. The Rev's desk was of mahogany; it showed a century's worth of dents and dings. There was hardly room on it for Reverend Paine to rest his elbows, it was so cluttered with loose papers, a stack of hymnals, a set of two bibles, the Old Testament and the New, with identical black bindings. Notebooks, pens, pencils, paperclips. Alongside the clutter was an old computer monitor and keyboard, and a gild-framed photo of a middle-aged woman. His mother, Tommy thought but didn't ask.

"My grandma, rest her soul," the Rev said when he noticed Tommy staring at the photo.

He continued, "I heard about the shooting the next day after it happened. Your brother called, wanting my help to identify the body." Light from the ceiling fixture reflected off the top of the Rev's head as he shook it. "He wasn't from around here, nobody in my flock knows him, never heard of anybody name of Willams. Williams, yes, tons of them, but Willams? Uh uh."

There were few wrinkles on The Rev's face, his skin was like smooth, smoked glass. The few wrinkles that appeared at the corners of his mouth Tommy interpreted as sympathy, and sympathy made him uncomfortable.

He said, "The St. Louis cops found an aunt."

"Yes, I spoke to her on the phone yesterday from somewhere in Missouri. Mrs. Adela Comptons. Nobody around here by that name, either. Poor soul, she wants to come claim her nephew's body, but has to scrape to come up with the money to buy a ticket on the Greyhound. I offered to wire her the money, but no sir. Pride, you know, A powerful thing, pride.

But why come so far, I put to her. At her age. Why not let us here in Pittsburgh handle the details? And the cost, which is considerable, by the way. Well, yes, was her answer, but Odell was the last of her line, except for herself, of course." He couldn't help chuckling at that. "I didn't suggest that her nephew might not have been worth such an effort on the part of an old lady, though I was thinkin' it. You bet your life I was thinkin' it."

Tommy's gaze came up from the floor for the first time. He said, "I've seen you marching. On the TV. I've seen you shouting, Black lives matter."

"Son, you've got that almost right, but not quite. All lives matter, not just black lives, all lives. Yours, too. The way I heard it, you had a choice, his life or yours, and you chose yours. Same as I would've, no doubt if, God forbid, I was in your shoes at that moment. Nobody wants to have t' make that choice, but nobody can fault you for making it."

"What if I told you that you didn't hear it exactly as it happened? What then?"

The Rev didn't always know what to say, but he had learned when it was best not to say anything. So that's what he did, he didn't say anything. He didn't bother saying that he wasn't Catholic and he didn't hear confessions. What was the point? Murdoch was so intent absolution, he would just ignore the Rev, go right ahead on and confess anyway.

Tommy decided to tell him, even though he had

promised that he wouldn't, what he had purposely left out of his statement to the police, omitted from every telling of the shooting incident to everyone except to Callahan.

Reverend Paine said, "The name Skruggs, I recognize. Charlie and his wife, Marna, and his kids, I know them, I don't know Michael. And who is this Callahan?"

"Actually, you might know her. She told me her father was white but her mother was African-American."

Reverend Paine shook his head, no. Scratched his broad nose.

Tommy went on to say that he had little choice, being off duty and with Bobbi, his beagle, on a leash, with no handcuffs and no cell phone, little choice but to allow his attacker to leave the scene. He had actually encouraged him to leave.

"But at the last moment, for some reason I don't even understand, I goaded him. Goaded him by saying, 'Be quick about it or I'll put some lead in that fat black ass of yours."

Tommy rubbed at his eye. He said to the Rev, "Callahan, my new girlfriend, she's a cop I met at Division 4 after the shooting. I love her, I think she'll marry me when I ask her, which I'm gonna do."

"And she's half black, and your best friend, Michael Skruggs, he's all black."

"Blacker than you, even." Tommy said, and afterward wished he hadn't.

The Rev was un-phased. "I think I understand. You wanna know where that ugliness came from. That bit of hate you didn't know you had in you. Hmm? That why you wanted to speak to me?"

Tommy shrugged, nodded. "Something like that, sir, yeah."

Reverend Paine said, "It happens, I do know where it came from." He paused for a second. "Remember out there behind the building, you flubbed that layup? I couldn't help thinking and almost saying out loud, 'White boys.' That's the place where it comes from, Thomas. That's where all the anger and all the ugliness comes from. From somewhere deep down inside the animal that is mankind."

Tommy said, "If it's inside us all, like you say, God must've put it there for a reason."

"Yes, but don't ask me what His reason was. I've come to realize that God's ways are not only mysterious but subtle. So subtle that a man can hardly notice, let alone understand the works of His hand. But you can be sure, there's a reason for everything."

"You're not saying it was intended that I shoot Odell Willams?"

"No, I'm not saying that, exactly. What I'm saying is this: we can't deny that there's a benefit for all the good apples in the barrel if by chance somebody comes along, picks the rotten apple out of the barrel and eats it. There's a reward for the good apples, they're rid of the rotten one, but what's the reward for the man that eats the rotten one? Most likely, a belly ache."

Somebody interrupted with, "Excuse me?"

A young woman, wide as the doorway and with rings in both nostrils, interrupted.

"Ms Dorita Scales, Thomas. She keeps me from being late for all my appointments. I should say she tries to."

"Which is what you will be, Reverend, if you ain't left here ten minutes ago."

"Oh, much as I hate to break this up, Thomas.... Say hello to Thomas Murdoch, Dorita, my friend Arthur Murdoch's little brother. I'll see you at the hearing Wednesday morning, Thomas. Hopefully we'll find time to talk some more, you and I."

At a surprising speed for a man of his age, Reverend Paine headed for the door, which his secretary had vacated. The Rev called over his shoulder as he departed:

"Her mama was munching on nacho chips when Dorita decided to get born. That's why her mama named her Dorita."

Then he was gone.

Dorita said, looking after him, "For a preacher, that man can lie like a rug."

CHAPTER 19

Morningside was a middle class neighborhood perched high on the East End bluff above the Allegheny River. Neat little houses on neat little lots. People there lived close together and managed to get along well enough: WASPs and Jews and Italians, and occasionally African Americans, too. The Charlie Skruggs family lived there in a neat two-story house of yellow brick with white faux shutters and a large front porch with a two-seater swing hung by chains from the ceiling. A neat front yard with a flower garden and raspberry bushes.

That evening, inside the house, a very festive scene was in progress, which struck Tommy as strange, considering that Thanksgiving was still three days away. The dining room was more than big enough to accommodate a massive breakfront that, according to Mrs. Marna Skruggs, was an heirloom from her mother's family, as was the mahogany dining table and a matching mahogany credenza.

That evening there were six around the table: Charlie was seated at the head of the table. He was as big a man as one would expect of an ex-pro footballer;

he was dressed for dinner in a brown suit and soft red tie. Seated opposite Charlie, when she wasn't on her feet serving, was his wife, Marna. She was formally turned out, too, in an off-the-shoulder dress of royal blue satin and a single string of pearls. Charles junior, age twelve, was wearing pressed jeans and a long-sleeve Steelers jersey with Polamolu on the back. And Sasha, age ten, who was going to be big like her dad, was all hair in corn rows—an hours-long project of her Mom's, no doubt.

The two other men were seated on the side of the table opposite the children: Michael Skruggs—Uncle Mickey—wearing a bib over a pajama top, his skin prune-wrinkled and ghastly. And to his right, a guest, Mickey's good friend Tommy Murdoch. Tommy helped Mickey by hefting his water glass and by cutting his meat.

Mickey tried to make light of the help. He said, "If I use up all my energy cutting my food, I'd be too tired to eat it. Ha ha."

Tommy couldn't quite put his finger on the festive nature of this meal or the undercurrent of desperation that ran beneath it—it was festive and tense at the same time. Was his presence at the table, with his ethnic mix, a cause of confusion for the kids? Was that it, or was something else at play? He seldom knew the answer to such questions.

The Skruggs adults knew of Tommy's family background. Mickey strove to explain his friend's mixed ethnicity to his niece and nephew, but he quit mid sentence, exhausted. Tommy took over.

He said, "My Jewish half won't let me eat ham, but my Catholic half loves it, so pass it, please. I'll have a second helping." Everybody laughed.

When the meal was over, Mrs. Skruggs made excuses for Mickey and tucked him into his bed in the guest room. The kids went off to their rooms to do their homework. Tommy thanked Marna for the lovely meal and the opportunity to spend some time with his friend. Charlie accompanied Tommy out to the curb and his car.

* * *

While Tommy was still with the Skruggs family, Callahan's shift at Division 4 had ended and she returned to her apartment.

There was no reason for concern, she thought, but failed to convince herself. She used the remote to shut off the TV. She couldn't concentrate on any program, nor could she concentrate on The City Paper or the latest issue of People Magazine. She began wearing a path in her living room floor.

He was a grown man, very grown. She had to smile to herself. Boyish in so many ways, but what man wasn't, and capable of handling himself in just about any challenging situation. God, yes. The man who attacked him with a switchblade knife found that out the hard way.

But the very act of killing a man had been quite an emotional setback, as it would be for anyone. And on top of that, learning that your best friend had cancer, and on top of that…

Yes, she blamed herself, too. She had fallen for him at first sight and like a ton of bricks. She had come on strong, probably too strong, adding to his cascade of emotional baggage. But she admitted she wouldn't do anything different if she had to do it all over again. No regrets. No reason for any. Tommy could handle whatever came his way.

Still. She checked her wristwatch. There's only so long a visit a cancer patient could stand, and only so much they could eat, and no matter how nice they were, only so much chin music Tommy could conduct with the Skruggs family. He should have arrived at her place by now.

She went to the window and looked down on the dark night and the light reflected from the utility pole across the way onto the cars parked on both sides of the street. One car sat idling. She spotted the red glow of its rear parking lights and an occasional puff of vapor from its exhaust pipe. Is that him? Why was he just sitting there? She ran to the front closet for a coat and threw it over her shoulders as she headed out the door. No time to wait for the elevator, she rushed down the stairs.

Yes, it was the Dart idling. Tommy sat behind the wheel, his chin on his chest. The driver side window was steamed. Callahan rapped on it, which seemed to startle him awake. He rolled down the window and turned his face to her; it was tear streaked, and his eyes were pleading.

"What is it, Sweetie? What's wrong?"

"He's dying, my friend Mickey is dying."

* * *

Charlie Skruggs had accompanied Tommy out to his car. Tommy had remarked that Mickey seemed in good humor. While his color wasn't good, he seemed a little stronger than...

Charlie was furious. He raged at Tommy, "Don't you know what terminal means? You idiot. He's terminal, inoperable, he's dying."

* * *

Relaying this to Callahan started the tears tracing new tracks down his cheeks.

"Poor baby," Callahan said. "My poor poor baby. This day has been too much, too f-ing much." She opened the door and helped him out of the car. Led him up to her apartment.

The night seemed endless and sorrow-filled for them both, but they spent it together on the sofa, she sitting up on one end and he curled up with his head in her lap.

CHAPTER 20

Large wet snow flakes swirled around the wind-swept courtyard between the big Murdoch house and Tommy's carriage house apartment. Callahan had called ahead, so when the Dodge Dart, with Callahan behind the wheel and Tommy looking glum beside her in the passenger seat, pulled in and parked, the whole family—Arthur, Nina, Edie, Madison and the beagle, Bobbi—had been expecting their arrival and came out to meet them.

As soon as Callahan was out of the car, the two girls were right there, while Bobbi made a point of hanging back. Callahan had been alerted to the possibility of a display of petulance toward her by the beagle. There was palpable tension. Tommy was used to Bobbi's occasional bouts of petulance. They were liable to occur whenever the dog felt her master had ignored her, didn't feed her on time or some other slight, such as Tommy being away all of last night.

Warned in advance, Callahan was not surprised when the dog refused to approach her. It did surprise her when the younger of the two nieces hung back as well. Callahan had insinuated herself into their lives, between Tommy and Bobbi and between Madison and her beloved uncle, and both dog and child were displaying their resentment.

Edie was feeling a little of that resentment, too, but she understood her role as older sister. She said, "Mads, don't…"

The parents finally caught up. Nina, knowing how much the little girl loved her Uncle Tommy, had been expecting something of this sort of behavior and had tried to get ahead of it. But failed to.

She said, "Maddie, honey, we talked about this, remember?"

The nine year old shook her head, no.

Edie, said, "Yes we did, Mads, we talked about this."

Having no experience with youngsters of any age, Callahan turned to Nina, who mouthed, I-G-N-O-R-E.

Arthur embraced his brother while at the same time leading him several paces away from the women.

He said, "We got the news about your friend Mickey. So sorry, bro. The Rev called to let us know. He really liked you, said he hoped you'd get to talk more another time."

"I liked him, too, Artie. You know, he was out shooting baskets behind the church when I got there. I didn't realize how old he was, but then I did the math. He must be near eighty, but man, he can still move."

Artie said, "You should've seen him like I did when he was young: working the key, fighting them for the rebound, killing them with that deadly hook shot of his." Artie could still see it when he squeezed his eyes shut. Then he shook off the vision, changed the subject. "Anyway, he said that old lady finally arrived from St. Louis, Willams's aunt…"

"Mrs. Comptons, I think the name was. The Rev said she was coming by Greyhound."

"Yeah, he said she's a sweet old lady, really. No anger, no axe to grind as far as he could tell. Evidently she means no harm, only wants to see her nephew buried with the rest of her family."

Tommy said, "In Saint Louis? She wants to take her nephew's body all the way back to Saint Louis, Missouri? I thought she didn't have any money. Didn't the Rev say that? You can't take a dead body on a bus, can you?"

Artie said, "Just for laughs, I'd like to see her try. No, they'll put it on a train. In a coffin, prob'ly, not a body bag. Her, too. On the train, I mean. Rev said his people were footing the bill. We should contribute to that, don't you think?"

Callahan, looking at her watch, called, "Tommy, you promised you'd drive me to work. I'm due to clock in at Division 4 in fifteen minutes."

It was at this moment that Tommy remembered his conversation with Sergeant McKenzie at the Police firing range. He started to say something to his brother, but changed his mind. Instead, he kissed his nieces and thanked them for taking such good care of Bobbi in his absence.

He then turned to his sister-in-law, Nina. He kissed her on the cheek and whispered to her, "We have to talk. Can we, after I take her to work?"

Nina's brow went up. Since when? she thought. Tommy had never confided in her or consulted with her, he always turned to Arthur. But she said, "Sure, Hon. Any time."

With a mollified Bobbi stretched out on the back seat and with Tommy behind the wheel now, the Arthur Murdochs watched until the Dart was out of sight.

CHAPTER 21

When Tommy returned from delivering Callahan to Division 4, he went strolling around the neighborhood with Bobbi. He had fences to mend with the petulant pooch, no doubt, and it was important to him that those fences be mended. He felt he and Bobbi were as close as man and beast could be. But just as important, he always found he could do his best thinking as he walked with her. So while the beagle was snuffling after the scents of squirrels, chipmunks and the occasional rabbit, Tommy was scratching for the right way to ask for advice from his sister-in-law.

Later that gray afternoon, he found Nina in her kitchen. He sat himself on a stool at the central island and watched as Nina spread peanut butter and daubs of strawberry jelly on crackers in preparation for the girls arriving home from school. Briefly the sun broke through the overcast and shone through the kitchen window to Tommy's side of the table, warming his face. Looking intently at him, Nina was reminded of the photograph of her mother-in-law that occupied a privileged place on Arthur's chest of drawers. The photo whose duplicate she had seen occupying a privileged place in Tommy's apartment, too—Irena Samuelson Murdoch, a raven haired, green-eyed beauty. How Tommy resembled her and how alike they were in many ways.

"You've had quite a week, haven't you," she said, giving in to the urge to run her fingers through his curly hair. "What with the shooting and your friend's illness. Not all bad, though. You found Elizabeth, didn't you? Or she found you. So not absolutely all bad."

Tommy sort of agreed, "No, not absolutely all bad." Although he didn't look as if he were convinced.

"But there was something you wanted to talk about. With me, not your brother?"

Tommy said, "A couple of things, actually." He took his time, looking as if he would never get started, but then he did. "Nina, If somebody had something of great sentimental value..."

"Uh huh?"

"...And that somebody wanted to give that something to another somebody, would that somebody want to wear that something instead of another something that somebody would pick out on her own?"

"I'm sorry, Tommy. You lost me somewhere between the somebodys and the somethings. But I got the 'her.' If you're referring to Elizabeth..."

"Yes, I was. I was thinking about Mom's beautiful engagement ring."

"Then our guesses were correct, it's that serious?" She considered him carefully, knowing his past missteps. "For both of you?"

"I'm not mistaken this time, Nina. Honest, I'm not."

"Then the answer is yes, Tommy. If I'm any judge of character, I'd say Elizabeth will be thrilled to wear your mother's diamond. You'll need to have the stone re-mounted, the old mounting is worn thin. But the stone is big and beautiful. She'll love it."

"And it's...where?"

"In the safe deposit box at PNC Bank, the one you share with your brother." Nina breathed a sigh of relief. That wasn't so bad. If only it were all that was on his mind. It wasn't. He still looked distressed.

He said, "There were always things best talked about with Dad, man things, at least that's the way it used to be when he was alive. I have to talk about those things with Artie, now. And other kinds of things, too. Um." He made a tight-lipped mouth and shook his head. "But there were always things I could only talk over with Mom. Now..."

Nina said, "I only got to know your Mom for a short time, Tommy, but I grew to love her. Arthur and I were only married a couple of years when she passed." She thought that over. "Two, to be exact. I was carrying Edie. She was so beautiful and such a dear lady. I loved her, too, Tommy, so if I can somehow substitute for her, well, I'd be honored."

He leapt to the point. He said, "I was hurting pretty badly because of, you know, the shooting. Still am, kinda. I feel like somebody kicked a chair out from under me and I'm about to fall on my ass. Sorry."

He took a breath. "Talking about it didn't seem to help." Talking about it with Callahan didn't seem to help, that was what he had been about to say to Nina, but he thought better of it. He said, "Elizabeth thought it didn't help because I was talking to the wrong people. She thought maybe I needed to talk to somebody who had been in the same boat, somebody who had, y' know?"

"Killed somebody, yes. Did she suggest somebody?"

Tommy nodded. "Yeah, she did. She suggested Sergeant Kenneth McKenzie."

Of course Nina had no idea who McKenzie was, Tommy had to tell her that he was the longtime chief of the Police Academy firing range, and that he had trained every police officer for the past ten or fifteen years in the handling of firearms. More to the point were the rumors whispered among Tommy's classmates at the police academy that McKenzie had put down three perpetrators or maybe six, or would Nina believe a dozen? Were any of the rumors true? Neither he nor Callahan knew for sure, but everybody believed them, and Callahan thought Sergeant McKenzie was the man Tommy ought to speak to. Nina wondered if it was wise to question Callahan's judgment. She did, anyway.

She said, "This McKenzie person... Pardon me for saying so, but he sounds really horrible, Tommy."

"You can say that again! And we were all scared to death of him. He was a very scary guy, then. Not so much now. He got old."

Nina nodded. She said, "Well, but if he helped... Did he?"

"If he helped at all, it wasn't by solving my problem. It was by giving me another problem. An even worse one."

Nina wasn't surprised to learn from her brother-in-law that Sergeant McKenzie had trained Callahan. After all, he had said that McKenzie had trained every graduate of the Police Academy, including Tommy himself, for the last ten or fifteen years. Nina figured from Callahan's age that she had been in uniform no more than two or three years, so of course McKenzie had trained her. She didn't know what to make of Tommy's quoting McKenzie as having said, 'Get her out of the cops before it's too late.'

"That's an exact quote, Nina, or as close to an exact quote as I can come. He said, 'She'll end up in a situation where it's kill or be killed, like the one you was in, Murdoch, and she won't shoot.' That's what he said, and if anybody knows, it's McKenzie. He said, 'She may even draw her weapon, but she won't shoot. She don't have it in her, that girl, she just don't.'

"Nina, what'll I do? How can I get her out of the cops before it's too late?"

Tommy's distress was obvious, and Nina was experienced enough with men to know that if they're seeking advice from a woman, they must be absolutely desperate. She never wished harder that her mother-in-law were still alive.

She said, "Have you considered the possibility that Sergeant McKenzie is just prejudiced against women being cops?"

Tommy hadn't, but now that he was led to think about it, maybe....

"Or the possibility," Nina continued, "that McKenzie is a psycho? If those rumors about how many people he's shot are true, he's nothing but a psychopath, and nothing he says should be believed. Not about Elizabeth, not about anybody."

"Huh. Then maybe my problem..."

"That's just it, dear. It was never your problem. At least, not your problem, singular. It was and still is your problem, plural."

"You mean..."

"Yes, dear. That's exactly what I mean."

* * *

From the time years ago when his and Artie's mother, Irena Samuelson Murdoch, was laid to rest,

Tommy had felt an ache that he would swear emanated from a hole that pierced his chest beneath the breast bone and extended completely through to his heart. The ache was so constant, he had learned to accept its presence, like heartburn after a big meal. He could go for hours hardly conscious of the ache until something or someone brought his mother to mind. Then he would discover that it was back, that it had not actually ever left. A sweet agony, a ghost of memory. His mother had been Tommy's guiding light, the docent on his tour of the world. She constantly challenged him to learn new things, to extend his reach, to broaden his horizons. And when he overstepped his limits, she was his shelter from the harshness of the world or the meanness he found in it.

Of course she was Arthur's mother, too, and being her first, Arthur commanded a preeminent position in the family. Irena loved and even admired Arthur, especially in the good looks and the clever, hale fellow, let-me-handle-this personality Arthur had inherited from his father. But Tommy and his mother were mirror images of each other, with their curly, raven black hair, eastern European complexions and dark green eyes that seemed to peer out at the world from a deep, exotic place. Besides which, Tommy was the child who needed to be mothered.

* * *

All this came back to Tommy now because for the first time he realized he might have misjudged his sister-in-law. Nina was a beautiful woman, a loving, attentive wife to his brother, the epitome of the helicopter mom to his nieces; she even paid occasional attention to Bobbi. But to him?

He always felt Nina tolerated him as if he were the baggage that came along with her husband, baggage she had to schlep as penance for loving Arthur. Tommy had always thought she was resentful of the role Arthur took so seriously, that of responsible big brother. He thought she resented the time and concern her husband wasted on him.

But hadn't Nina just proved him wrong? Tommy could still feel her fingers in his hair. Amazing the warmth the woman could generate with a simple touch, just like his mother used to. Nina had known just the right thing to say. Not to tell him what he ought to do, but to simply lead him to a fork in the road where the correct path might be chosen, then let him do the choosing. Just like Mom used to do.

Not a problem singular, but a problem plural? Yes. Thank you, Nina.

* * *

As he left the main house he noticed the light was fading, as it did that time of year, making it five o'clock, give or take. Two days before Thanksgiving, he realized. The air nipped at his ears, like Bobbi's love bites. Thinking of Bobbi, she needed fed and walked before it was time to pick up Callahan at the end of her shift. Bobbi would want to wear her snug plaid jacket this cold night. Tommy felt light as he mounted the carriage house stairs.

CHAPTER 22

Officer Liz Callahan and her partner, Officer Joe Lee Gordon, were cruising in their black-and-white on a routine patrol of the Brown's Hill area on the far edge of Division 4. Officer Gordon was at the wheel. They were about to request a meal break when their comm unit started squawking at them:

ALL UNITS. A DOMESTIC DISTURBANCE. 5700 BLOCK OF SOLWAY. APPROACH WITH CAUTION. RESIDENT THREATENS VIOLENCE.

Solway was near the station house. They knew they would not be the first unit to get there, but Callahan grabbed the mic to respond; Gordon hit the siren.

As they sped along Beechwood Boulevard Callahan yelled over the screaming siren, "D.D.'s are rare in our bailiwick. Be careful, Joe Lee, please. D.D.'s are dangerous."

Joe Lee yelled back, "Tell me about it."

Three vehicles had already arrived when they got there, one of theirs from Division 4 and one from Division 5 were blocking ingress into Solway from both directions. There was a third black-and-white, that one from Division 6. The officers were barricaded behind it, weapons in hand. One of the officers from 6 had a portable p.a. unit.

A group of citizens was gathered on the sidewalk in front of 5722 Solway. It was the type of residence that was typical of Solway Street: a 3-story red brick house, newel-posted wooden porch, lots of gables and chimneys, neat front yard.

One elderly woman, gray hair, wearing an apron over a housedress, old-lady shoes, was more frantic than the others in the crowd. She spotted the female officer and hustled over to her.

She cried, "Thank God you're here, officer. Help, oh, help, please. They're gonna hurt my Bennie. He's not dangerous, he's just out of his head. Temporarily."

Her husband had shoved her out of the house, locked all the doors and was threatening to kill himself. When questioned, some of the neighbors were shocked—Mr. Stein was the nicest old man, never a bit of trouble, not like some around here. Others were not at all surprised—senile old man, nuttier than a fruitcake. Yeah, Stein was the name.

Benjamin Stein. He came home from work in a blinding rage, announced that he'd been furloughed. Those sons of bitches at UPMC didn't even have the guts to fire him, they furloughed him.

"Same thing," said one woman in the crowd, then they all agreed, it was the same thing.

He threatened to kill himself.

"A gun? Where would my Bennie get a gun? Oy, heaven forbid." Mrs. Stein had passed frantic and was approaching hysterical.

Officer Gordon reached for his Sig Sauer, and Mrs. Stein clawed at his arm. She pleaded with him, "Don't hurt my Bennie, please. Don't hurt him."

Officer Gordon, weapon in hand, signaled his partner to arm herself and join him behind the barricade. Callahan said to him, "I don't think we should handle it that way, Joe Lee. Not in this case."

"Wait for a Swat team?"

"Not that way, either. I think, this way." Without further thought, she unbuckled her weapons belt and laid it on the hood of the black-and-white. With only her comm unit in hand, she walked up to the front stoop, mounted the stairs onto the porch.

Her C.O., Lieutenant Craig, yelled at her, "Liz, no…"

She called out, "Mr. Stein? Mr. Stein, my name is Elizabeth Callahan. I'm a police officer. If you'll look out here, you'll see I'm not armed. I've got my walkie-talkie in my hand, nothing else. I want to come in so we can talk. Okay, Mr. Stein? I want to come in and talk."

A voice from inside, sounding old and weary and frantic, replied, "I'm through talking. I'm sick and tired of talking. I'm gonna kill myself. Get off my porch. I got a knife, a...a meat cleaver, and I'll use it, I swear."

What had she been thinking? Once on the porch, Callahan realized she had violated all the rules, placing herself in harm's way. But she also realized it was too late to re-think the situation. One thing sure, she would catch hell from Lieutenant Craig, no matter the outcome.

She drew in a chestful of air, hoping there was courage in it, and called, "No, Mr. Stein, I'm not getting off the porch and you're not gonna hurt anybody. I'm coming in and we're gonna talk. You wouldn't hurt a girl, would you? Okay, Mr. Stein? I'm coming in and we're gonna talk."

There were sirens screaming; Lieutenant Craig was cursing and yelling about veteran officers who pull rookie stunts; other official vehicles were screeching to a halt on the street in front of the house.

Officer Callahan spoke into her comm unit, "Sorry, Lieu. I've come this far, too late to turn back. I think I've got this handled. I'm goin' in."

And she did.

CHAPTER 23

Tommy pulled up in front of Division 4 at six o'clock. The night was as dark as Callahan's dark blue uniform. She stood in the ground floor lobby awaiting his arrival. He could see her standing behind the glass front door, silhouetted by the lobby's blue-white fluorescents. She was still in uniform, of course, and wearing the regulation black leather jacket over it. Her shift was finally over, Thank God, but Lieutenant Craig's snarling reprimands were still drumming painfully against her eardrums. Tommy realized he'd been holding his breath. He let it out noisily.

Callahan climbed into the Dart, leaned over the gear level and planted a wet kiss on his cheek.

She said, "Right on time as usual, Sweetie, and thank god. I needed to get out of there, and I'm dying for a latte."

"How was your shift? Routine?"

She rolled her eyes and made a so-so gesture with a hand that he wasn't able to see in the dark. She said, "Well…no. There's no such thing as routine in our business. Never a dull moment, actually."

After a while Callahan was able to struggle out of the cocoon of noise her c.o.'s shouting had forced her into. That's when she noticed that Tommy seemed calmer than she'd expected him to be, it being the evening before his hearing. She wondered if things had gone well with the interviews of Reverend Paine and Sergeant McKenzie. They must have gone well, since he seemed less stressed. A lot less stressed than she was at the moment. She asked about the interviews, but he put her off by asking if her craving for a latte had a destination attached to it: Starbucks, Duncan or Crazy Mocha? They were all open and nearby. She let him choose, so Crazy Mocha it was.

They carried their lattes to a two-top by the window that faced onto Murray Avenue. Apparel shops, art galleries, framing shops, all were in the process of closing, their storefront lights winking off. But ice cream emporiums and restaurants of every conceivable ethnicity predominated there, so the street was busy with traffic pulling in, pulling out, passing, and the sidewalks were crowded with diners coming and going. You'd think it a holiday atmosphere if you were a stranger to this neighborhood. But Elizabeth Callahan, who worked there, and Tommy Murdoch, who grew up there, both recognized the scene they were watching from the coffee shop window as just the usual for Squirrel Hill.

Though Callahan was worried for Tommy, she noticed he continued to appear fairly well composed, as if he had begun to make peace with himself. If he was still tangled up in disturbing emotions, he didn't show it. She thought it surprising, but she decided not to say anything until after they had both enjoyed several swallows of their drinks. Instead she reached across the table, took his hand and kissed it.

He wiped a frothy mustache off her lip and said, "I missed you so much all day."

She thought she could eat him up.

She said, "It's only been a few hours, silly, but yes, I missed you, too. Sometimes a few hours can seem like forever." Then she brought up the subject of the interviews. She watched him shrug. She said, "Something must have helped, you don't look nearly as stressed. You look more, well, more at peace than I've ever seen you."

Tommy did feel more at peace. As amazing as that was, he had an explanation for it. But it was complicated.

Tommy told Callahan that he went to see Sergeant McKenzie at the Academy firing range thinking that he had two problems to worry about: one, he was hurting from having killed someone; and two, his best friend, Mickey Skruggs, was dying of cancer. He learned from the sergeant that instead, he had a third problem to add to problems one and two.

He chose to avoid discussing in detail problem three with Callahan at that particular moment, since it concerned her and was very complicated. Later for that.

He skipped to his visit with Reverend Paine at his church in Homewood. He told Callahan that he had arrived there thinking he had three problems, one, two and three, but he learned from the Rev that he might be harboring, somewhere deep in his body or soul, a prejudice against black people, a source of hate that he hadn't been aware of.

Tommy said, "So I started the afternoon with two problems, but now I have four. See? That was my afternoon. Great, huh?"

"Geez, Tommy, how do you come out of that less stressed? Seems to me you oughta be more stressed."

"You'd think so, but I have an explanation. But it requires some math."

"Uh uh, Sweetie. I don't do math, no way."

"You're just like my mom, she didn't do math, either. Try, okay? I'll try to be clear. Stop me if you need to."

Tommy had taken into consideration his entire life, from childhood through elementary and high school, through his semesters at CCAC, through the Police Academy and the City police force, his transfer over to the County force at his brother's behest, and finally to his present position as County Detective. His entire life.

He said, his eyes wide with discovery, "I realized, and this is amazing, I realized that I had never ever had more than just one problem to worry about at a time. Isn't that amazing? And lucky? So many poor bastards have a shitload of problems all at once. Excuse the French. But they do, they lost their job and there's no money and the rent is due and the baby is sick and there's another one on the way and the car won't start and and and. But not me. I never had more than one worry at a time."

An instantaneous re-think of her own life led Callahan to wonder if she weren't in the same boat as Tommy on that score.

She said, "Sweetie, I'm sort of with you so far, but I'm wondering where the math comes in."

"Right now. I figure, the amount of worrying that any one person is capable of doing is a finite number; no more than that finite number of worrying is humanly possible. Okay, so far?"

"So far."

"For our discussion, it's not necessary to assign an actual amount to it, an empirical number will do. Say the total amount of worrying that is humanly possible is X. Okay?"

Callahan scratched her cheek and knitted her brow. She said, "X. You're not gonna tell me that Y is something else, are you? You'll lose me, I promise."

"No, no. Just X. It's not that hard, Hon, honest."

He touched her brow, trying to erase the confusion lines.

"If you only have one problem at a time, like I've

always had before, you do all of that worrying, X, on one problem and that can be an awful lot of worrying. But if you're lucky enough to be able to spread X out among four problems, your worries are reduced to ¼ of X, which is a hell of a lot less to worry about." He made a gesture with his hands equivalent to a tada!

Just in time, Callahan put down her latte to prevent spilling it all over the table. At first, she thought she was going to lose it, then she knew she already had. Starting with a giggle, then a hahaha, then in a moment she had to grip the table to prevent falling off her chair onto the shop's carpeted floor.

Tommy, though, was serious. He said, "What's so funny? Tomorrow morning at 10 o'clock is the hearing to determine if I keep or lose my badge, whether the shooting of Odell Willams was justified or not, but I'm a lot less worried about it because I've got so many other things to worry about. I simply did the math."

"Oh, stop. Please, you're killing me."

He did, and Callahan finally regained control of herself.

She said, holding her sides, "You know, it worries me that you have so many talents, like math, that are far beyond my reach."

He said, "I've got another worry. I can picture you in a white wedding dress with a veil and a long train. So beautiful. I'm worried you're gonna want to get married in your uniform."

CHAPTER 24

Wednesday morning was damp, overcast and bone chilling, but since Tommy was only ¼ X worried, he decided not to take the weather as an ill omen. Which proved to be justified, for when he stepped into the ground floor media room of the Public Safety Building, he was able to breathe a sigh of relief.

It was a large rectangular room, longer than wide, rather like a movie theatre only with a level floor and un-tiered plastic seating. There was a low stage in the front, two steps up, with a set of flags in each corner: the U.S. and the Commonwealth of Pennsylvania flags on the left, the City of Pittsburgh and the Bureau of Police flags on the right. A long table set with five chairs, all facing front, occupied center stage. The sole object on the table at present was a judge's gavel. At stage right was a court stenographer's setup.

The rear of the media room was reserved for and equipped for, of course, the media, and to Tommy's relief he saw that although the print media was fully represented, he saw several TV camera crews in place but no on-camera talent. Tommy might briefly find himself on the 6 o'clock and 11 o'clock TV news broadcasts, but no interviewers were present to shove a microphone in front of his face. He had dressed in his best suit, the one his Mom used to call bar mitzvah blue, for nothing. He smiled about that now.

There were a lot of people milling around, most of whom were either well known to Tommy or recognizable. Easiest of all to recognize by far, because of the brass on his hat and the epaulets on his shoulders, was Police Commissioner Anders Andresen. Hovering around him were Captain Paul Barancovich of Internal Affairs, who would conduct the hearing, and Lieutenant Barney Craig of Division 4, Callahan's boss as well as the boss of detectives Goldberg and Michaels, who were here to testify. The detectives were standing to the side, keeping their own company, appearing anxious to avoid the brass. Tommy also spotted Sergeant McKenzie. He wondered what McKenzie was doing there.

There were two women present that Tommy recognized from previous on-the-job contacts: an Assistant Medical Examiner, whose name Tommy couldn't recall; the other was Judge Sikora of Family Court division. There were also two women in the company of Reverend Paine, one of them an old woman that Tommy assumed was Mrs. Comptons, the deceased's next of kin. The other woman was maybe Mrs. Payne—Was there a Mrs. Payne? Tommy didn't know—or maybe she was a parishioner of the Rev's, come along to care for Mrs. Comptons. The old lady had come a long way and she looked as if the journey had nearly killed her. The Rev never left her side, his huge body hovering protectively over her.

A young man wearing a green corduroy sport coat and a wool plaid tie took a seat at the stenographer's station and nodded at Captain Barancovich. Barancovich in turn signaled the commissioner and the judge. The three mounted the stage and took seats at the central table. Barancovich took the gavel in hand, then didn't seem to know what to do with it. He looked at the judge; the judge took the gavel from him, rapped it once sharply on the table and handed it back to him. Barancovich shrugged, banged the gavel once again. It worked—everyone scurried to a seat as if they were in a game of musical chairs.

"First order of business..." Barancovich's voice sounded as if it were filtered through an ashtray full of cigarette butts. He was interrupted by Judge Sikora, who whispered in his ear. He said, "Oh, yeah. The hearing into the shooting death of one..." He consulted his notes. "One Odell Willams is now in session." He nodded at Judge Sikora.

"First order of business, I got to thank Commissioner Andresen for arranging the details of this hearing, above and beyond the call of duty, so to speak, in lieu of District Attorney Murdoch's recusal of himself and his entire staff. For obvious reasons, I might add.

"Other thanks go to the Honorable Jubal Cahill, President Judge of Common Pleas Court, who let us borrow Judge FayeDean Sikora from the Family Division to make this hearing extra official. Also, Judge Cahill lent us Mr. Smalls, there, Court Stenographer, for which we're eternally grateful.

"I understand we also owe thanks to the FBI for the identification of the deceased, and to Saint Louis, Missouri, P.D. for providing us with his rap sheet, which is long as yer arm.

"Well now, I think I've thanked everybody that needs thanking…" This time it was the Commissioner, sitting at Barancovich's left elbow, who interrupted him and whispered in his ear. "Oh yeah. Thanks go to Reverend Duvall Paine and the folks from the First Church of the Redeemer for seeing to Mrs. Comptons, the deceased's next of kin. Now?" Everyone agreed, those were enough thanks.

Then Captain Barancovich informed those present that it was his intention to conduct the hearing as informally and with as much dispatch as possible, so they all could as quickly as possible get back to doing their job, which was to serve the public. Judge Sikora had agreed that it was perfectly legal for him to run the hearing informally, as long as an official version was produced in the standard form. For the record. A nod toward the stenographer.

"To that end," Barancovich said, "Everyone in the room please stand up and raise your right hand." Everyone did. "Do ya? Say, I do. Now siddown. Consider yourselves sworn."

Judge Sikora rolled her eyes, but voiced no objection.

Once Captain Barancovich got started, it was clear he wasn't kidding about dispatch. First he called the two plainclothes detectives, Goldberg and Michaels. Very plain clothes, Tommy observed, recognizing the wrinkles in their suits as the same ones he saw the afternoon of the shooting. Maybe that was intentional on their part.

"No need to come up, fellas," Barancovich said as they stood. "Just stand where you are. Remember, you're already sworn."

They answered, yes, when Barancovich asked if they had arrived on the scene shortly after patrol officers had cordoned off the area.

Goldberg added, "We got there about the same time as the meat wagon." That went over big with the audience.

The detectives also answered, yes, to confirm the fact that they had examined the scene thoroughly, and, yes again, to confirm that they returned to Division 4 and took County Detective Thomas Murdoch's formal statement. Finally when asked if they had discovered anything at the scene or anywhere else that contradicted Mr. Murdoch's sworn statement, each of their answers was, no. They were done testifying; Barancovich told them to sit.

Next the Assistant Medical Examiner was called and was also told to stand in place rather than step forward. The Assistant M.E. was a small, dark woman who reminded Tommy of his fifth grade teacher, the one who used to smack his wrist with a ruler when he fumbled a math problem with fractions.

"Dr. Atkins," Barancovich addressed her, "I take it you thoroughly examined the body of the deceased?" She had, both on the scene and more thoroughly at the morgue, where she personally conducted the post mortem. "For the sake of brevity, Doc, could you skip the technical stuff and just tell us if you found anything, either at the scene or in the morgue, to contradict Mr. Murdoch's sworn statement as to what occurred last Tuesday afternoon?"

It was obvious the Assistant M.E. was not happy about skipping the technical stuff, but she lacked the courage to defy Captain Barancovich, gruff as he was. She said that she found nothing inconsistent. She was thanked and told to sit.

After a brief conference, Sikora and Barancovich nodded at each other and Barancovich said, "We call Allegheny County Detective Thomas Murdoch. Stand up, will you, Murdoch."

Tommy stood. He felt the eyes of everyone in the room on his back.

Once again Barancovich referred to the copy of the incident report that was on the table in front of him. He said, "Now Detective Murdoch. This here is your sworn statement of what occurred on the afternoon of Tuesday last. Do you still swear to it?"

Tommy thought, As far as it goes. He said, "Yessir. Yessir, I do."

"Is there anything needs to be added to it?"

"No sir, not…not anything."

There was a palpable sigh of relief that blew through the room. Tommy wasn't sure whether he only heard it or actually felt it. Either way, it was evident everyone in the room was as eager as he to get past this unfortunate incident. If that was possible to do.

Barancovich said, "Well then, you can siddown." But Tommy didn't sit down. "You got something more to say?"

Tommy nodded. "It won't take but a minute."

He took up a part of that minute just staring at his hands. He finally said, "I'm grateful to everybody here. Since the…incident, as you call it, since then, people have been pretty decent about not treating me like a killer just because I…uh, I shot Mr. Willams. But people were puzzled why I got so turned upside down over a guy like him, a guy with a long, violent record, a guy who would've killed me if I didn't get him first.

"Well…I heard it said that shooting a man changes you. They don't say how it does, only that it does. Well, let me tell you, it does. Um. When I was going through the Academy, Sergeant McKenzie told my class, like he prob'ly told every class:

'Before you start carrying a gun, better give some thought to what you might have to do with it.'

"Well. Like everybody else in my class, I didn't give any thought to it, not until it was too late. I don't like what I did with it, even though I had to. I never intended to hurt anybody, let alone kill them. Life and death is God's work. I didn't like doing God's work. I'm not even sure God likes doing God's work."

Tommy stopped rambling and sat down.

Barancovich huffed noisily through his nose, but he was pleased when he checked his wristwatch. He said, "I don't see any need for any further testimony..."

Judge Sikora cut him off.

She said over him, "...but since we're operating informally and there's no real hurry." She looked daggers at Barancovich. "If anyone has anything to add to the record... How about you, Arthur? Your recusal notwithstanding."

At his seat in back near the media area, Arthur climbed to his feet. "Nothing to add, Your Honor, not from me. But I think Reverend Paine is trying to get your attention."

Indeed he was. The Reverend stood, which never ceased to generate O's as he eased up to his full height. He said, "Mrs. Adela Comptons of St. Louis,

Missouri, would like a word or two, if you please, Judge."

Barancovich, trying to regain control, chimed in with, "By all means, by all means."

The old lady left Reverend Paine's side and came up the center aisle toward the front, walking as if she didn't trust the task to her legs. She stopped when she was within an arm's length of Tommy, who had re-taken his seat in the front row.

That close to her, Tommy could see that her skin was the color and texture of a worn out leather football, and her wiry gray hair had been braided into corn rows that had begun to unravel. She was dressed in what Tommy had always called a housedress. This one might have been red once, with little yellow flowers, but had faded nearly to purple.

She had a sad, sweet little girl's voice.

She said, "I hadn't in mind to say anything, just to bring my nephew home and lay him down beside his Mama. Had to, since my dear sister is with the angels and couldn't do it her own self. No blame on her, my sister deserved better than Odell for a son. Odell was trouble from first to last; his father, the same, his grandfather, him too. Ain't been a decent man in the Willams family for three, four generations."

She turned to Tommy with doleful eyes. "Honey, the Reverend say you're a good boy, not a hateful bone in your body. And I believe it. You listen to me now, hear? You stop your grieving, stop it right now. Forget Odell Willams. He made you do what you had to. Hear what I'm saying? You stop your grieving now."

Slowly she opened her arms to him; he rose and stepped into her embrace.

* * *

"Congratulations, Detective," Artie said as he embraced his brother.

Marge Tangretti handed Tommy a bundle that turned out to be the leather wallet that contained his badge and County Detective's ID, and his revered weapon, the H&K in its leather belt rig.

She said, "Elizabeth sent them over from Division 4 with her special congratulations. She figured you'd want them back as soon as it was official."

It took a moment for Tommy to realize Marge was referring to Callahan. When it finally dawned on him, he broke into a smile. He put the ID wallet where it belonged, in the inside pocket of his suit coat over his heart. The holstered weapon he held in his hand and stared at it as if not knowing what to do with it.

He said, "I guess I'll have to re-learn to live with this." He slipped it into a side pocket. He said to his brother, "I've got so much catching up to do. I'll be back on the job first thing tomorrow morning."

"Jesus, no," Artie said. "No, bro, not tomorrow."

Marge took hold of his arm. She said, "Sorry, Hon, but you've got...you've got a funeral to go to tomorrow."

"Charlie Skruggs called the office first thing this morning. Your friend passed away in the middle of the night. In his sleep."

"Huh?" Tommy shook his head. "Not Mickey. In his sleep? Mickey? No. Not... He wasn't hurting, was he?"

"He's done hurting, pal," Artie said. "He's done."

CHAPTER 25

ttention! Possible B & E 5418 Glenway. Recommend Silent Approach.

* * *

A silent alarm generated a loop of robocalls, from the possibly-invaded residence to Alarm Central and from Alarm Central to Division 4. Officer Liz Callahan and her partner, Officer Joe Lee Gordon, hustled to their black-and-white. Pedal to the metal, though they didn't have far to go: 5418 Glenway was literally around the corner and four blocks down. No siren. Silent approach. Joe Lee leapt out of the vehicle even before it was completely stopped. He eased cautiously toward the front door. Callahan ran around to cover the back, her weapon drawn.

There was an elaborate back garden, an arbor, a stone path. Some slushy snow on the grass in the center of the garden, some icy patches in areas of shadow. A big picture window looked out on the garden. A hole the size of a basketball was blown through the window. Callahan approached the window, peered through the hole into what appeared to be a den or

TV room. Bloody feathers all over, some still adrift on currents of air from the hole. Diamonds of glass throughout the room caught ambient light from the moon and twinkled it back at her. In the center of an expensive looking Middle Eastern rug, the bloody carcass of a large brown bird. A pheasant or grouse, poor dead thing. Callahan holstered her weapon, called for Joe Lee to stand down.

* * *

Callahan and Gordon were now back at Division 4, answering telephones, typing up incident reports, occasionally responding to calls, filling in where possible for those officers whose presence had been required at Tommy's hearing and had not yet returned to duty. Callahan particularly got a kick out of sitting behind Goldberg's desk in the Homicide squad room. She had ambitions.

But as three o'clock and the end of her shift drew near, Callahan felt herself growing more anxious. She had never been in love, not like she was in love with Tommy. Flirtations in the past, yes, school girl crushes, sure, but not this longing to be in Tommy's embrace with his powerful arms around her. Not this desire to go up on her toes to gaze into the kaleidoscope of his glowing green eyes. But to somehow help him to find comfort in the face of losing his best friend? She felt terribly inadequate. In the past she had always needed to show a tough exterior, and had never before been cast in the role of comfort giver.

She wasn't sure she knew how, while Tommy was like her father, God rest him —strong and resourceful and brave, but still able to be sensitive, well, sort of, and childlike. A girl could lose a guy if she couldn't help him over a rough patch.

What added to her anxiety was a phone call from Nina Murdoch earlier that same afternoon. It started out innocuously enough.

Nina said, "First order of business, since we're going to be seeing a lot of each other, we've got to settle on what I should call you. Callahan is out and that's my final word on that subject."

Yes it was, she thought. It seemed as if it had taken forever to convince her colleagues in the police department to stop calling her Callahan. Once she finally got her partner to call her Liz, the other guys followed suit. It was a tough habit to break, seemed like everybody in the cops called each other by their last names. But as of last Tuesday, calling her Callahan was forever reserved for Tommy.

She couldn't help wondering if, some day, she would be able to call Nina, Sis. She had always wanted to have a sister.

"Are you still there?" Nina asked. "You have to decide: Elizabeth, Liz, Betty, Betsy, which? Your choice."

She chose Elizabeth.

"Okay, that'll work for me. Elizabeth it is. The girls may have other ideas.

Nina continued, "Now, in the tummel of the last couple days…"

Elizabeth wondered if she had heard correctly. She said, " Tummel? What's tummel?"

"Hang around long enough with the Murdoch brothers, you'll find yourself using words they picked up from their mother. Yiddish words like tummel. It means what it sounds like. Tumult. In the tumult of the last few days…"

Elizabeth said, "Actually, tummel sounds like more fun than tumult."

"I agree. Anyway, I'm sure the boys have forgotten that tomorrow is Thanksgiving."

"Omigosh. I did too."

"I'm not surprised. Anyone who doesn't have to stuff a twenty-one pound turkey is liable to forget Thanksgiving. Some day you can call me on the phone and remind me it's Thanksgiving. I'll be glad for an invitation, and even more glad you had to stuff the turkey instead of me."

"You don't know how wonderful that idea sounds to these ears, Nina."

"Anyway," Nina said, "Your assignment for to-morrow, around five-ish by the way—not sooner, please—is to see that Tommy shows up with you for Thanksgiving dinner. He has probably forgotten all about Thanksgiving in the tummel of the last few days. Okay, Elizabeth? And do your best to see that his mood is not gloom and doom. It's a holiday, for chrissake."

CHAPTER 26

It was a few minutes past three o'clock when Tommy came through the door into the reception area of Division 4. Callahan was there waiting for his arrival. He looked really down.

She said, "There's my superhero, right on time."

He said, "Superhero? Yeah, well, it takes a while to get into these tights and this cape, but here I am."

Actually, he was still dressed in the suit he had worn that morning to the hearing, with the addition of several of Bobbi's hairs on the pant legs. That beagle never could resist a guy in a bar mitzvah blue suit. Tommy thought of it as his funeral-go-to suit. Everyone who worked in law enforcement had a lot of funerals to go to.

Glum as he was, Callahan had to admit she had never seen him so well turned out: the suit, light blue oxford cloth shirt, muted tie, a high shine on his black brogues. She said, "You clean up pretty well, Detective. But don't I get a smile, not even a little one?"

Tommy didn't feel much like smiling, but he managed one for her. What he really wanted was to be in the comforting shelter of her arms, but the duty sergeant was looking on from his perch at the reception desk. The sergeant was mocking Tommy, making faces with Groucho Marx-type bouncing eyebrows—Tommy's cheeks turned red as beets.

Callahan had been admiring the way his green eyes looked striking against the blue suit. She was wondering if she could convince Tommy to wear his hair longer, maybe collar length in back. That would look absolutely stunning.

She kissed him on one of those red cheeks and said in a stage whisper the desk sergeant could hear, "Ignore Sgt. Rafferty and his monkey faces. He'll never grow up."

She zipped up her leather jacket against the wind's late afternoon bite and they went out to the Dodge Dart. It was warm inside, but Tommy sat frozen behind the steering wheel.

He hung his head and said, "What am I gonna do?"

"Well, first you'll drive over to my place so I can change out of my uniform into something more appropriate. Then we'll go to the funeral home."

He managed to look at her.

He said, "Visitation is at McNeel's in Homewood. I know the place, it's right around the corner from Reverend Paine's church. He's prob'ly doing the funeral tomorrow."

"Not tomorrow, Hon," Callahan said. "Tomorrow is a holiday. Thanksgiving, remember?" So Nina was right, he hadn't a clue. "I expect the actual funeral will be Friday or Saturday. Maybe even Sunday."

"Friday, Saturday, Sunday." Tommy shrugged. "What difference does it make? What am I gonna do?"

"I don't know. Maybe… Would you like to try playing What if?" He looked at her. "What if. Like, what if your friend Mickey wasn't dead. What if it were you that died and Mickey was alive. What would you tell him to do?"

"I wouldn't tell him anything, I'd be dead."

"Come on, silly, what if?"

"Well…"

Callahan could tell by watching Tommy's eyes that he went away for a while to a place where he had stored memories.

He said, "I remember something Mom told me when Dad died. That was… I was fifteen. It was right after the priest concluded the prayers of resurrection or absolution, something. Anyway, Mom said, 'The only chance Dad has of living on is if we live on.' And she was right, Dad does live on, in a way, since I remember him."

Callahan said, "Good advice, I think. Mickey will live on because you live on. Not very Catholic, though, is it?"

"No, but Mom was Jewish, remember? I am, too, sort of."

She hadn't forgotten.

* * *

There had been no sun to speak of all day, only a leaden sky. The lasting light was fading fast as they pulled into the parking lot adjoining McNeel's Funeral Home. The weather forecasters were threatening snow and the temperature hovered near the freezing mark where it usually hovered when the heaviest snows fell in western Pennsylvania.

Tommy was surprised to find the parking lot nearly full. Mickey was a friendly-enough guy, to be sure. He had undoubtedly made many friends and lots more acquaintances among the faculty and student body of CCAC. But that many? He wondered about that to Callahan.

"Aren't you forgetting about his brother? Charlie was famous once, wasn't he? And he must've had so many teammates over the years. Some of these people may be paying their respects to Charlie as much as to Mickey."

* * *

One hundred fifty years ago Homewood was one of the ritziest, if not the ritziest neighborhood in Pittsburgh, and most of the multi-storied, multi-chimney-ed, multi-gabled mansions in Homewood reflected the tastes of the well-to-do of that time. A century and a half later, however, those people were long gone and their mansions were shadows of their former selves. Some of them listed badly left or right, ships in a rough sea, and some were gone, torn down, their lots weedy and derelict, looking like missing teeth.

Situated in between two such missing teeth, McNeel's stood alone on the northeast corner of Homewood and Brushton Avenues. It was an old pile but not in the typical style of that place or that past era, being of white clapboard instead of mortar and brick, and being meticulously, painstakingly cared for instead of derelict. It looked as if it had been dragged from New England to squat like a curiosity in Homewood.

Three members of the McNeel family stood in the vestibule, just beyond the front door, to greet arriving mourners: The proprietor, Augustus McNeel, was a short, bespectacled, dark-skinned man who looked as old and as wrinkled as God himself. His tuxedo coat looked a tiny bit large on him, as if Augustus had begun to shrink. His children, twins, son Carson McNeel and daughter Carolynne McNeel Forbus, had outgrown their father in height and width, but otherwise the resemblance was strong. The daughter, Carolynne, was the taller of the two siblings. Her abundant black hair was piled on top of her head and secured with a gold buckle. She moved gracefully in her black business suit, encouraging arriving guests to move right along inside, herding them as efficiently as an experienced traffic cop.

Some people looked as if they were born into their professions. They said that about cops, Tommy thought, and they could say that about the McNeels—they looked born to be morticians.

They were helped off with their coats and were led by Carson McNeel into what he identified as 'the Great Mourning Room.' It was certainly great: an ornately decorated rectangle long enough and wide enough for Charlie Skruggs and his old teammates to play a game of football. Three walls were papered in soft gold tones, the carpeting that covered most of the floor matched the gold papered walls, and the rows of folding chairs that occupied one corner of the room either were valuable antiques or at least they resembled valuable antiques. One of the longer walls was mirrored, which surprised Tommy until he realized that McNeel's was not designed with Jewish traditions in mind.

Tommy spotted a few white faces; he recognized some of them—a City Councilman, a restaurant owner, an exec from PNC Bank, a few faculty members from CCAC. As expected, though, most of the mourners were African American, and scanning those, both men and women, Tommy judged their ages to be approximately the same as Charlie's: no longer young but not yet old. Their obvious affluence and their obvious athleticism told Tommy that Callahan had been correct: a lot of Charlie's old teammates and their significant others had shown up to pay their respects to Charlie. He hoped Mickey didn't mind.

* * *

Charlie and his family—perhaps in deference to the tender age of Charlie's daughter—were lined up to greet arrivals near the entrance to the Great Mourning Room rather than near the coffin. Tommy was glad he had dined with them the previous night and that he was able to remember their names—Mrs. Marna Skruggs, Charles Junior and little Sasha—and was able to introduce them to his girlfriend.

Callahan was able to sense the emotional fragility of the man whose arm she clung to, still she couldn't help being amazed at how comfortable Tommy was in that gathering. When she mentioned this to Tommy, he shrugged.

Tommy had noticed the collection of ornate antique folding chairs when he first entered the Great Mourning Room. They had been unoccupied then, and despite what he guessed were a hundred mourners present, those chairs were still unoccupied. Everyone was standing, talking not very quietly, occasionally laughing until it came to mind where they were and why. It seemed to Tommy that most people purposefully ignored the coffin or simply pretended it was empty. It didn't much matter, Mickey was ignoring them, too.

With Callahan maintaining a constant reassuring grip on his arm, Tommy wound his way through the conversational groupings of mourners. He introduced Callahan when he encountered someone he knew, but he kept moving forward, determined to reach his friend. To say goodbye.

The coffin was of walnut with antique brass hardware. Mickey was asleep inside it, looking as if he preferred not to be disturbed. He was dressed in a gray suit with a thin maroon pinstripe and unfashionably wide lapels. He might have been rummaging around in Artie's closet, Tommy thought. Then he remembered he had been along when Mickey bought that suit, helped him pick it out, the occasion being Tommy's graduation from the Police Academy. Seldom worn, that suit. Mickey was never comfortable in it, let alone in a dress shirt and tie. Strangely, Tommy thought, Mick looked comfortable enough in it now.

$$* \quad * \quad *$$

The R.I.P background music faded off.

A voice was heard to say, "May I have a word?" Reverend Duvall Paine.

Positioned to the right of the coffin was a narrow speaker's dais. The Rev lifted it effortlessly, as if it were made of balsa wood, and moved it more toward center stage. He took his place behind it and waited for silence—he didn't have to wait long. No one had to be told who he was.

The Rev was wearing a suit of bar mitzvah blue, Tommy noted. It saddened him when he thought he couldn't get any sadder, that he couldn't share that bit of humor with Mickey.

* * *

Reverend Paine said, "Considering the fact that tomorrow is Thanksgiving, the family wishes to delay interment till Friday noon. Now, everyone knows how fond I am of cemeteries, which is not at all. Consequently my graveside ceremonies tend to be quick. Fact, quicker than you can say Kareem Abdul Jabbar."

That being the case, he informed the crowd of mourners, they would gather right there in the Great Mourning Room on Friday at noon.

"At that time I will do some preaching, that's inevitable, and some eulogizing, that too, on Michael Skruggs. But I didn't know Michael. You folks, at least some of you folks, did know him. So we'll take as much time on Friday noon as we need to, no hurry at all, so anybody that wants to can come up here and tell us a story or anecdote about Michael. Something you remember about him, it can be funny or sad, either one, no matter. That's the best way, in my way of thinking, to give Michael a good head start on his journey forward."

The Rev asked everyone who knew Michael to take a few minutes while they were enjoying Thanksgiving with friends and family to prepare what they'd like to say on Friday noon. Then he offered some advice:

"At my graduation from seminary...oh yes, they did, they took pity and let me graduate," he said, his gaze spanning the crowd, sharing the humor. "The great Reverend Ralph Abernathy, of the SCLC and

Martin Luther King Jr.'s right hand man, he was invited to attend, and he did us the honor of doing just that. He said some words to us graduates. We were about to go out into the world, he said, to preach the gospel. To tend a flock, he said. He put a question to us at that time, 'What is it that is the hardest thing about being a preacher? That was the question he put to us. No, he said in answer, not that and not that and not this, that or the other thing. The hardest part about being a preacher, Ralph Abernathy said, is trying not to get mad at God and blame Him for all the mean, cruel, senseless, disastrous things that go on in this world. In this vale of tears.

"My friends, while you're thinking about Michael Skruggs: if you happen to stumble on how hard it may have been for that young black man to make his way in the world; if you happen to think about a young man with most of his life ahead of him falling victim to cancer; if you wonder at the pain he had to endure in the last days of his life; then it is Reverend Abernathy's advice and my advice as well—try your best to cut God some slack. Okay? Try not to get angry at Him, it may not be His fault. Bad things happen, good things happen. We don't have answers to why they do, they just do. For all we know, there may be a good reason, we just don't know it." He sadly shook his head and shrugged his massive old shoulders. "Until Friday noon, then…"

Reverend Paine departed the Great Mourning

Room, followed shortly by other mourners, a few at a time.

CHAPTER 27

To thank the mourners as they departed, the Charlie Skruggs family did the reception line in reverse, with the daughter and son at the head of the line, both of their young faces tear-stained—they so loved their Uncle Mickey—followed by Mrs. Skruggs and finally, Charlie. Tommy and Marna Skruggs searched each other's sad faces and hugged, but exchanged no words. Charlie's handshake was less crushing this time around—he looked weary.

He said to Tommy, "I'm sorry about the other night. I'm sorry I called you an idiot. I didn't mean it. I felt... in a way I think I was jealous of how close the two of you were."

"Forget it, Charlie, I have. I know how much Mickey loved his big brother. Me, too."

They hugged. That is to say, Charlie wrapped his linebacker's arms around Tommy and engulfed him.

Tommy looked back to see Callahan and Marna Skruggs deep in conversation. He wondered what those two had to say to each other. Then he saw the Rev talking in the foyer with, who else? His brother Arthur. Not surprising really, Artie somehow managed to know everybody who was anybody in Pittsburgh, the Rev and Charlie Skruggs included.

Tommy was no shrimp, by any measure a sizable young man, but once again he watched as once again his hand disappeared into Reverend Paine's huge paw.

The Rev said, "You'll drop by my church another afternoon, won't you, Thomas? We had a nice little chat, you and me, but like most talks with me, it was interrupted."

Tommy promised that he would, then turned to his brother. They hugged, and in the process Artie managed to frisk Tommy.

Artie said, "You're not carrying, Detective? You know the rules, you're supposed to be carrying $24/7$."

Tommy spoke emphatically, in other words, too loudly. "Fuck the rules, Artie." The curse echoed in the confines of the foyer. Then more quietly, "Fuck the rules. I don't consider myself on duty till…Not till Monday, and I'm not carrying until then." He didn't add that he wished he never again had to carry, but he thought it. For the first time since he graduated from the Police Academy, he didn't miss the weight of his H&K.

He looked around for Callahan and saw her whispering again, this time with Reverend Paine. He wondered about that, too.

* * *

Then they were back in the Dart waiting for their turn to pull out of the parking lot. Callahan had taken his hand as they stepped out into the night. She had to let go when he helped her into the car, but she took possession again as soon as Tommy was behind the wheel.

As the Dart crawled through the lot toward the exit to the street, Tommy realized he had no idea which way to turn, and he didn't feel much like asking.

Callahan beat him to it. She said, "Go left, back to my place." He did, he turned left. She added, "There's a CVS on the way, stop there. We need to buy you a toothbrush. And anything else you might need. You're sleeping at my place tonight."

Tommy failed to respond. He didn't know what to say, nothing seemed like the right thing to say.

Callahan continued, "That Marna Skruggs is a wise woman. Knowing how close you were with Mickey, instead of being just worried about her own family, she was worried about you. The way she talked about you, I'd swear you were a nephew. She told me I shouldn't leave you alone tonight.

"Reverend Paine said pretty much the same thing, only couched in biblical terms that I really didn't understand. Something about Lot's wife and a pillar of salt?" She shrugged. "But isn't it great when people advise you to do what you intend to do anyway? I don't intend to leave you alone, Thomas Murdoch. Not tonight, not ever."

Tommy said the only thing that seemed appropriate.

He said, "Okay."

Up ahead he spotted the huge sign for the CVS. He clicked on the turn signal and pulled in.

CHAPTER 28

The heavy drape over the window denied light access to Callahan's bedroom. Tommy couldn't tell if it were late night or early morning. There was a clock radio whose face he couldn't see on the single nightstand on Callahan's side of the bed. His watch was where it usually was, on his left wrist, but he couldn't see his watch, either. He was flat on his back, with Callahan's head resting on his left shoulder, his arm pinned to the mattress beneath her body, and her beautiful left breast—he couldn't see it except with his mind's eye, the round pink nipple puckering to his kiss—her beautiful left breast pressed against his chest.

He didn't want to wake her and he didn't want to move, ever again. He was suddenly amused, tried not to laugh as he thought of the CCAC wrestling coach, a man Mickey had tagged with the name Buster Bee—Tommy wasn't sure, but he thought the man's name was actually Brinkbain. Anyway, Buster Bee used to hunker down on the mat next to a pair of his wrestling trainees, usually one or the other would be flat on his back, pinned the way Tommy was now.

Buster would slam his palm on the mat—'One! Two! Three! Yer out!' Tommy had lost the wrestling match to Callahan. He was pinned, couldn't move and didn't care to. Everything was perfect...except Callahan's soft, black hair was in his face; it tickled, and he was afraid a sneeze would wake her.

Callahan stirred.

She said, "Did you sneeze? Bless you, if you did. Wha time zit?" Her breath was morning damp and warm against his neck. She smelled of sleep and sex.

Tommy apologized for waking her.

He said, "You okay?" She hadn't moved off his chest; it didn't look as if she intended to. He hoped she would and at the same time hoped she wouldn't.

"Umhm. You?"

"Me? What could be wrong with me, I got laid last night."

"Like, a couple of times, as I recall."

" A couple of times."

Tommy was quiet for several minutes, thinking.

He said, "I guess it's always like this, I mean, things good and bad coming at the same time. I shoot and kill someone and I meet you. Like that. I remember being told that Dad's parents were killed in a car crash the same week that Artie was born."

Callahan lifted her head off his shoulder.

She said, "What a pleasant thought for first thing in the morning. But, yeah. My Dad died the very same week I graduated from the Academy."

"Really? Jeez. Mine died when I was fifteen. Nothing good happened after that." Tommy seemed to stumble over his next thought. "I can't think of a thing good that happened when Mom died, either. Something's wrong with my theory, maybe things good and bad don't always come together."

"You loved her so much, Tommy. I wish... I'd like to have at least met her."

"Artie was the first borne, long before me. Ten years before me. Jewish families, even half Jewish families, celebrate the birth of the first boy as if it were some kind of a miracle."

"Catholics are no different, believe me."

"There were two...Mom called them misses, between Artie and me."

Callahan said, "Oh, that's sad. But I'll bet the two misses made your arrival seem like a miracle."

"Yeah, I was her favorite. Mom always called me her special child."

Callahan yawned.

She said, "You hungry? I'm starving."

"I can't tell, I'm numb from the neck down." But when she tried to move, he prevented it.

She said, "I've got to pee."

"Me, too. You first." He let her go and watched her butt as she wiggled off to the bathroom.

They eventually showered in Callahan's phone booth-sized shower stall, then they dressed and had coffee and toast. They retrieved Bobbi from her crate in Tommy's carriage house apartment, fed her and walked her around the neighborhood. Bobbi kept getting tangled up in her leash and tangled among their legs. She knows, Tommy thought, she knows.

It was cold but windless and bright. They felt a need to walk, and a need to rehearse. Later that day they would be seated across the Thanksgiving table from his two precocious little nieces. If they were to avoid embarrassing questions about sex, they would have to pretend that last night hadn't happened.

They looked at each other, wondering, Did it show? They needed to rehearse.

CHAPTER 29

The Thanksgiving celebration at the Murdoch home turned out to be a huge success. It began at six o'clock when Tommy and Elizabeth Callahan arrived with an apology from Callahan for showing up in uniform. They had drawn straws at Division 4 and luckily—or unluckily, depending on how you looked at it—she had pulled the third shift, 11 p.m. to 7 a.m. It turned out, though, that Tommy's two nieces couldn't get enough of her. They were much more impressed that she was a real police officer, not just a crossing guard, than they were that their father was District Attorney or their uncle was a County Detective. She wore a real cop uniform.

Uncle Tommy and Bets—in the middle of a game of Scrabble the girls started calling her Bets instead of Elizabeth, and without anyone making a tzimis out of it Bets stuck to her. She and Tommy concluded that those two precocious schemers had decided on that name ahead of time. Anyway, the youngest niece, Madison, won the Scrabble game. No one willingly admitted that they had let her win. Instead, they accused her of cheating and everybody laughed.

Before Nina called them to dinner, Tommy punched the Skruggs's number into his cell phone. Charlie answered; he sounded surprised Tommy had called.

Tommy said, "You're gonna call me an idiot again."

"I am? Why?"

"Because I called to wish you and your family a happy Thanksgiving. Despite…everything, happy Thanksgiving, Charlie."

Tommy listened to the sound of cyber silence for a few moments. There was a sigh that sounded like a shrug before Charlie finally replied.

He said, "Things are what they are. No…I don't think you're an idiot. Not at all, Tom, and I'm glad you called. Happy Thanksgiving to you and your family, too."

* * *

Tommy was sure eating one more bite of Nina's delicious turkey dinner would cause him to explode. Everyone at the table heard him say as much. But then Nina cut large wedges of pumpkin pie and squirted whipped cream on a particularly large wedge. She announced, "This one's got your name on it, Tommy."

He couldn't resist. He swallowed the first bite and the girls shouted, "Boom! There goes Uncle Tommy!"

* * *

Tommy delivered Callahan to Division 4 at eleven o'clock and promised to pick her up again at the end of her shift.

He said, "Let's go to breakfast at Ritter's or the IHOP, my treat." They were his favorites, but he had an ulterior motive that he tried to toss out in an offhand manner. Still, it came out as a plea. "You can help me decide what to say at the funeral service."

"Will there be time for me to change, do you think? After breakfast? I'd rather not go to the funeral in cop clothes."

"There will be time, don't worry about that. I were you, I'd be worried about staying awake. You haven't slept in twenty-four hours."

"I suppose you have?" Callahan giggled. "Neither one of us did much sleeping last night. But don't worry, I'll be fine. I don't have to speak at the service. If I fall asleep…you wouldn't abandon me there, would you? The idea of falling asleep in the Great Mourning Room…brrr. The thought really creeps me out."

She kissed him and climbed out of the car. Tommy watched her butt as she walked into the building, seeing with his mind's eye her butt wiggling out of bed that morning.

He sighed, slipped into drive and headed home.

CHAPTER **30**

The night had turned mean. The wind seemed determined to give Pittsburgh a good shaking, and the moon hid in fear under a blanket of cloud. It may have been that way earlier, but Tommy noticed it only after he was back in his apartment. It was so quiet. Except for Bobbi resting comfortably in her crate, he was alone. For the first time that day, he was alone.

Feeling emotionally and physically drained, he spent his last strength on whisking off his bar mitzvah blue suit. He would need to wear it again to the funeral. He hadn't washed, hadn't flossed or brushed his teeth, had only plopped onto the bed in his underwear. He knew he wouldn't be able to sleep, wouldn't be able to sleep, wouldn't be able to...

Suddenly a rhythmic tapping on the bedroom window scared the wits out of Bobbi—she darted out of her crate and leapt onto the bed at Tommy's feet. The noise scared Tommy too, but as usual the H&K was on the nightstand beside the bed. With it in hand and the safety in the off position, he tiptoed to the window to investigate—it was Mickey! He had somehow shimmied up to the window and was tapping on it to get Tommy's attention. He raised the window and Mickey scrambled in.

Boy, was Tommy glad to see him. They sat side by side on the bed and laughed and teased and poked at each other playfully. Tommy remarked on the meanness of the night and that, if it continued, it boded poorly for the funeral due to take place in a few hours. He asked Mickey if he thought it would be better for a funeral if it were freezing cold and windy, maybe even snowy, or did he prefer it to be a little warmer and rainy?

Mickey said, "Far as I'm concerned, either way is okay, long as you do the dying instead of me." They had a good laugh over that.

Tommy woke up laughing, but Bobbi was staring at the window and growling, with her back up. The rain continued its rhythmic tap tap tapping on the bedroom window. The night seemed to have made the decision for them, the funeral would take place in the rain.

CHAPTER 31

Of the choices of restaurants Callahan had been given, she chose the IHOP, knowing it was Tommy's favorite breakfast place. However, once inside and looking around, she wondered what about that place appealed to him. The red plastic banquette-style booths showed small gashes repaired with duct tape, and the Formica table tops were sloppily wiped and sticky to the touch. Maybe he liked the fact that there were four flavors of maple syrup to choose from on each table in cutesy little carafes.

The diners that morning proved to be mostly blue collar working men in jeans or denim coveralls and ball caps with team logos. They fidgeted, impatient for their meals. They killed time browsing the front page of USA Today or staring at their cell phones or staring at wall posters that declared, Kids eat free on Sat-ur-dee, or touted, All-you-can-eat Spaghetti Nite every Wednesday, $8.99. What in the world could explain the big grin on Tommy's face? The syrupy sweet smell of the place and its kitchy '50s look? Oh, well. He loved the IHOP, so Callahan was resigned to loving it, too.

If there was a hostess, she was occupied elsewhere. Tommy led Callahan to a booth near the front window. She sat, careful not to rest her arms on the sticky table top. A tired-looking waitress, working hard on a wad of chewing gum and carrying a steaming carafe and two coffee mugs, approached their booth. She was wearing a faded yellow uniform, its skirt fronted by a small, used-to-be white apron. Support hose were doing the best they could for her varicose legs. She greeted Tommy familiarly, calling him Honey. Over the left breast of her uniform top was a tag that ID-ed her as Prudence. Callahan took her name as a caution against the food. Tommy introduced the waitress to Callahan, calling her Pru, and introduced Callahan to Pru as his girlfriend.

Pru said to Tommy after giving Callahan's uniform the once-over, "For a minute there, Honey, I thought yinz were under arrest. So, you're the girlfriend, huh? Well, take good care of this guy, but don't ever give him breakfast. I need him here, he's my biggest tip-per." Neither Tommy nor Callahan got as big a kick out of that as Pru did, herself.

Tommy's bar mitzvah blue suit was the next target for Pru's jaundiced eye.   She tsk-ed and said, "Who died this time?" When she was told the deceased was Mickey Skruggs, she said, "You mean your friend? The…uh, the black guy you're always with? Ah, that's tough, Honey, real tough. Sorry."

Then the serious questioning began: Did they want

Belgian waffles or pancakes? If pancakes, what kind and how many, a tall stack or a short? Bacon or sausage? If sausage, links or patties?

Pru warned Callahan off her first choice of strawberry pancakes.

"Nuh uh, Sweetie, not today," she said, leaning in close to keep her words just between them and to give Callahan a whiff of the JuicyFruit gum she was chewing. "I had a peek at the strawberries back in the kitchen. Them suckers got curly hair. Better go with the blueberries."

She landed the hot coffee carafe on their table and left, leaving them to pour for themselves.

Callahan never thought herself a particularly classy act, but she knew a dump when she was in one, but she thought it best not to comment. She thought Tommy ought to know better, but he seemed right at home.

* * *

Tommy asked her about her night, had her shift been a busy one?

She said, "Was it ever. Busy isn't the word. Crazy would be more like it." That wasn't the reply Tommy expected. She explained, "We were short-handed because it's a holiday. Put that together with a windy night. We have so many private homes with alarm systems, more than any other division in the 'burgh. The wind blows open a door that's not well latched, that sets off the alarm and we get a call from Alarm Central."

"Isn't Alarm Central supposed to call the resident?"

"Not when the resident is basking in the sun in south Florida. No, Division 4 gets the call, and Joe Lee and I… You met my partner, Joe Lee Gordon? Off we go to investigate. Is it the wind or a real B.I.P." Tommy remembered from his days on the City job, B.I.P. meant burglary in progress. Callahan went on, "It's kinda… unnerving. The houses are always pitch dark and it's the dead of night."

Tommy was imagining it: There was Callahan advancing stealthily toward a darkened house, Sig Sauer drawn. He couldn't help linking that with what Sergeant McKenzie had said about her not being able to shoot at a critical point. Tommy had managed to push Sergeant McKenzie's warning into a tiny compartment in the attic of his brain, hoping to store it there until a more convenient time, such as after the funeral. But now…"

Then he was aware that Callahan was waving a hand in front of his face. "Where did you go? You were a million miles away."

"In case you can't tell, I'm feeling swamped. There are so many things we need to discuss and so little time, and so many distractions."

As if to prove that point, Pru showed up with their meals. Their annoyance must have shown because she said, feigning a huff, "Well, excuse me." The plates landed on the table in front of them, and Pru stomped off.

Tommy ignored it. "Most pressing, of course, is, what am I gonna say this afternoon about Mickey?"

"Right, but the other stuff you were referring to, stuff we need to talk about? You mean personal stuff? About us?" Tommy nodded. Callahan said, "Well then, I suggest we talk about one right now while we're eating." She chose that moment to pop a forkful of blueberry pancake into her mouth and was surprised how good it tasted. Was there something to the IHOP after all, or was it just that she was ravenously hungry? She said, "Pick an easy one to discuss while we eat, then we'll tackle your speech. Deal?"

Tommy was more than pleased to tackle an easy one rather than the one he feared to tackle. "Deal." A little Belgian waffle, a bite of link sausage. "We need to discuss an engagement r…"

"Stop right there, Tommy Murdoch. If this is a proposal…If you plan on proposing to me here in the IHOP, my answer is no. I swear I'll say no."

"No no, that's not what I had in mind. A ring, we need to discuss an engagement ring. It's just that I'm a lousy shopper. I can't handle a jewelry store, and I was wondering if, that is, if I had one that was of sentimental value to me. It's a beautiful ring, really. If you wouldn't mind…"

"If you're referring to your mother's engagement ring, if it is so beautiful, I'd have thought your brother would have given it to Nina."

"No, Mom was still living when they got engaged. She danced at their wedding. She was still wearing it. The ring, I mean."

"Oh, well then…"

"Nina says it would look gorgeous on your finger.   According to her, the mounting is very old and worn thin, but the stone… She said it's a beautiful blue white diamond, and big, too. She thinks it would be perfect for you. It and the matching wedding band are in the vault at the PNC branch on Forbes Avenue."

"Well then…"

"You'd wear Mother's ring? Whew. I was worried you wouldn't want to wear somebody else's ring."

"I would, Tommy. If it's your mother's ring we're talking about, you bet I would. With a new mounting, of course, but yes, I would. And it'll bring us years and years of good luck. You bet I would. And don't look at me that way. And no proposals. I won't be proposed to in an IHOP, I've got my pride."

He promised he wouldn't.

*   *   *

He checked the time and was relieved to find they had more than an hour before they would have to leave for Homewood. He considered those hours precious, because he really needed help. Callahan saw his distress. She knew a lot of people feared public speaking worse than death. She had no such fear herself, the reason being that no one had ever asked her to deliver a speech and the odds were good that no one ever would. So why worry?

Some nerve, her about to give advice about speechifying, never having done any. However, she remembered that on the occasion of her class's graduation from the Police Academy, Lieutenant Commander Alitha Garvey, Callahan's idol in the force, not counting her own dear father, told the class as she began her address that they could relax, because she vowed not to violate the three cardinal rules of public speaking. Then Lt. Commander Garvey proceeded to tell the class what those rules were. Those were the very ones Callahan intended to pass on to her lover.

She said, "You don't have to be told word for word what to say."

He didn't? Tommy wasn't convinced of that.

"No, you don't. You were Mickey's best friend, you'll think of something simple and to the point. I have confidence in you. You just need to keep in mind the three cardinal rules of public speaking, and you'll be fine."

"Three cardinal rules. What are they?" And why did Paul Simon's Fifty Ways come to mind?

"Number one: Don't lose sight of the intended subject of the speech." Callahan said, "For you, that translates into, it's not about you, stupid. It's about Mickey."

"It's about Mickey, not about me. I get it. Okay, number two?"

Callahan said, "Number two: Keep it short."

"That will be easy. Three?"

"Rule number three is last but not least. It goes like this: No, no, stupid. When I said short I meant really really short. Keep it really really short, and the audience will love you."

CHAPTER 32

Western Pennsylvania can usually be trusted to provide the worst kind of weather for a funeral, but with that Mickey Skruggs was in luck. The previous night's wild winds had scurried off to the northeast, dragging with it the pelting rain and menacing clouds. It was still bitingly cold—it was nearly December, after all—but it would not be a surprise to see sunglasses perched on frost-nipped noses.

There was something inherently absurd about a funeral on a sunny day, but then Tommy thought maybe all funerals were inherently absurd, one way or another.

He pulled the Dart into McNeel's parking lot. As expected, they were met by the blackly-clad twins, Carson and Carolynne. But then another one of McNeel's men, also in formal black—Tommy wondered if he was Mr. Forbus, Carolynne's husband—approached the Dart and tapped on the driver's side window. When it had been lowered, the man leaned in and asked, "You folks are Mr. Murdoch and Miss Callahan, right? Thought so. Don't pull your car in line behind the hearse. You guys get out here, I'll pull yer vehicle out of the way over yonder. Keys'll be in the office when you get back from the cemetery. The Skruggs family would like you folks to ride with them in the limo."

"That's sweet of them, don't you think, Tommy? A real honor for you," Callahan said.

If Tommy hadn't spent the night in Callahan's arms, if he had wakened to the kind of morning western Pennsylvania usually conjured up for a funeral, if his shooting of Odell Willams had not been judged to be justified, if his and Callahan's future didn't look so bright, if, if, if. Yes, if all that weren't so he might have wept at Charlie's thoughtfulness. As it was, he had to blot his eyes to clear his vision. What popped into his head at that moment was that for years he and Mickey had been dead wrong about their big brothers, and that Mickey was so right to have changed his mind about Charlie. Tommy wanted to find Charlie right away and tell him so.

They left the Dart in capable hands and went into McNeel's.

* * *

Overnight a change in the Great Mourning Room had taken place. The longest wall of the room was made up almost entirely of windows. Tommy hadn't noticed this Wednesday night because the windows had been hidden behind ceiling-to-floor length drapes of heavy green brocade. Now the drapes had been drawn back to allow the sun into the room, and it became less a funerary viewing room and more a sitting room in the Palace of Versailles, only at that moment the occasion was an audience with Michael Skruggs, not King Louis the Fourteenth.

There were fewer mourners, too, Tommy noticed, and the mood of those present had changed. Today they really were mourners. There was less chatter and that only in hushed tones, and less bling. Fewer gold neck chains and other expensive jewelry. Less trendy clothing. Folks were dressed for warmth—it would be cold where they were going. And there was no milling around; everyone was seated and squirming. The antique folding chairs were ornate, but they weren't comfortable.

Tommy, holding Callahan's hand, led the way to the front row where the Skruggs family were seated, close to the speaker's lectern and the coffin. The Skruggs daughter immediately attached herself to Callahan, talking to her in whispers. Charlie drew Tommy away from them, toward the coffin. Tommy thanked Charlie for including him and especially for including Callahan.

Charlie nodded toward the rows of mourners.

He said, "They act as if loud talk will wake him."

"He does look so peaceful, like he's sleeping."

"You'll help us carry him?"

"I loved him, Charlie. I'd carry him on my back if I had to."

* * *

Reverend Duvall Paine emerged from the clergy lounge, ducking his head to clear the top of the door frame, and took his place at the speaker's lectern. On the way to the lectern, he stopped at the casket and paused over its contents. He's still in there, Rev, Tommy thought.

The Rev was wearing a simple black cassock over a black vested suit. The buttons of the cassock were left unfastened; the ends took wing with each of his graceful movements.

Tommy thought most of the people attending that afternoon had closer ties to Mickey than did Wednesday night's crowd, but also they were more familiar with the Rev, his physical presence and his reputation as an orator. His arrival at the speaker's lectern brought the mourners immediately to silence and attention.

The Rev's voice had to have traveled a long way to finally reach his mouth, Tommy thought. It was deep and resonant, and everything he said sounded not only wise but familiar, as if Tommy had heard the words before but was pleased to hear them again.

* * *

The Rev said, "Those of you who join me every Sunday at First Church of the Redeemer know of my fondness for the Book of Genesis. Those folks whose stories are told in that Book are so much like us. They're so real, so dysfunctional, just like us, that I can't help but love them. Take Adam and Eve for instance. What a pair of screw-ups. Not one brain between the two of them, I think. They're progenitors to each and every one of us, but I swear, what a pair of screw-ups. I'm convinced God only created them because He was desperate. He was lonely, you see. Wandering around in the vast, empty universe He had created, and it was good, He'd said so, Himself. Good, maybe so, but there was nobody to talk to. So God created Adam and Eve—His first try at human beings, an experiment with a sad result, I'm afraid.

"Then He created the Garden of Eden—paradise—the perfect place where they could hang out all day, eating and drinking the fruits of the vine, maybe playing games of Scrabble, just talking, chewing the fat, so to speak. The three of them, God, Adam and Eve, hanging out in Paradise. Imagine. Everything they wanted would be immediately at hand, and anything they didn't want to be there would just simply not be there. And anything they wanted to know they would somehow get to know. There would be no unanswered questions. That to me would be paradise."

The Rev turned away from the mourners and strode—two strides was all it took—to the casket. A quick glance, then back to the lectern.

"As I said the other night, I didn't know Michael Skruggs, but in the past several days I've spoken to many people who did know him, and they all said essentially the same things: He was a good young man, Michael was, who loved his family and they loved him. He was a hard worker with a good job and good prospects for the future. He had lots of friends, one special friend in particular, a white man—if that doesn't tell you something about both of them. Michael Skruggs, in short, had a smile for everybody and was trouble to nobody. Why, then? is the question."

The Rev slowly panned the mourners, as if expecting someone among them to attempt an answer.

"Why, then?" he repeated. "Well, we know how that story in Genesis goes. God had great expectations for Adam and Eve, but they just didn't measure up. They got kicked out of the Garden into the real world where they had to struggle to feed their family; where they had to suffer pain; where there were lots of questions but no answers."

Reverend Paine looked around at the casket, then back again. "Why, then? Why, when on every street corner in our neighborhood there are young men, no better than thugs, doing bad things? Why, when in our opinion justice would be better served if one of them were to die? Why, instead, take Michael Skruggs?

"I got news for anyone who asks: Homewood is no Garden of Eden. We are up to our necks in the real world and seems as if we still don't measure up. Sad but true, we don't. As a consequence, we suffer constant pain, we struggle daily to feed our families, and everywhere we turn we are faced with questions for which we have no answers.

"As people of faith, however, we are bound to believe that Michael is now in a better place. Where he is now there is no struggle, no pain to suffer, and finally, no unanswered questions. Paradise. That is our prayer for him. Can I hear an amen?"

He did, he heard a loud chorus of them.

CHAPTER 33

Next, the Rev called Charlie Skruggs to the lectern, granting him the honor of first eulogy. Charlie rose from his chair in the front row and advanced without hesitation, offering his hand to the Rev. There were at least four decades of difference in their ages, but the two very large men, the ex college hoopster and the ex pro footballer, stood with hands clasped, powerful, confident gladiators. But then the Rev took a seat, leaving Charlie to face the rows of seated mourners alone. Standing with his back to his brother's casket, Charlie's confidence took flight and there was panic on his face. He fumbled in one inner suit coat pocket, then the other one, searching for notes he had prepared and for his reading glasses, too. He couldn't find either thing. With a curse under his breath, he gave up the search.

He said:

"When it came clear a couple weeks ago that Michael was losing his battle with cancer, in my desperation for something to say, I told him what my coaches used to tell me: Life is like a game of football, Michael, I said to him. You win some and you lose some. That had always sounded wise, to me. Michael just laughed and said, 'Have you forgotten how lousy I used to be at football? Guess I'm no better at living.'

"Of course I remember how bad he was at football. It was the most frustrating thing in our childhood. Here I was, the captain of every team I played on from PeeWee League to the NFL and everything in between, and my brother, my accident of a little brother—yeah, Dad admitted to me once, Michael was an accident—my little brother couldn't qualify to carry the water bucket. He was born with ten thumbs and two left feet. He was so clumsy, it was embarrassing. What I'm saying, he was so clumsy it embarrassed me."

It was too much for Charlie. Tears tracked down his face and dripped onto the elusive notes that were on the lectern where he had misplaced them.

He said:

"I used to beat up on my little brother because he frustrated me. Guess I always bullied him. Michael said he forgave me for that and I believe he meant it. Yes, I have to believe he meant it."

Charlie might have gone on to say more, but his wife, Marna, decided he was done. She took him by the arm and pulled him back to his seat.

* * *

The Rev hurried to the lectern, blaming himself for the dark cloud that hovered over the room. He had hoped people would relate pleasant memories; he hadn't meant to turn the Great Mourning Room into a confessional.

He scanned the rows of mourners, searching for the right somebody to call up next, somebody likely to alter the mood. Ah, there. The very person was seated to the right of the weeping Charlie. The Rev beckoned to Charlie's daughter, Sasha.

The sight of the ten year old, wearing a dark blue, knee length dress with a bodice trimmed in black velveteen, the sight of her youthful face, did indeed alter the mood. Smiles and nods of approval filled the Great Mourning room.

Callahan wondered how Marna Skruggs had managed to find such a lovely dress for a pre-teen so quickly, one that didn't make Sasha look as if she were on her way to a kid's birthday party. The internet, she supposed.

Tommy, mistakenly thinking he would be called to the lectern after Charlie, sighed, grateful for a few minutes' reprieve.

It was obvious to the mourners that the girl had given serious thought to what she was about to say— she had a note card in hand. But Sasha knew what she had written on the card; she never referred to it.

She told the mourners that Uncle Mickey always made time for them whenever he had a day off from work. He would take her and Charlie Jr. places when Daddy was too busy. Places like, for instance, the petting zoo in Highland Park to visit the lambs and goats.

"That was when we were little," Sasha said. "When we got older, Uncle Mickey used to take us to the big zoo."

He took them across the Allegheny to the Children's Museum on the North Side, and when they were old enough, he took them to the Science Center and the big Carnegie Museum in Oakland. And to Carnegie Library, he often took them to the library.

"Lots of times Uncle Tommy would come along, too," Sasha said. "He's not really our uncle, but Uncle Mickey said it was okay to pretend."

* * *

It was the perfect segue. Reverend Paine called on Tommy.

In preparation for his turn, in addition to Callahan's advice about keeping it short and keeping it about Mickey, Tommy had given a lot of thought to what his father—successful lawyer, power broker in the City Democratic Party, frequent after-dinner speaker—had said to Tommy after he had flubbed an audition for membership in his high school's Rhetoric Club:

Always prepare in advance, Thomas, never try to get away with winging it. And remember, when you're in the spotlight, you're not a teacher, you're an entertainer.

Tommy didn't know if he believed the part about being an entertainer, he didn't think he had it in him to be an entertainer. But his father's advice and Callahan's, too, were keeping him afloat as he stepped to the lectern.

He said:

"Last night my sleep was disturbed by a tapping on my bedroom window. I got out of bed and went to the window to investigate. I looked out. It was Mickey! What a shock, I thought he had died. But no, somehow he had managed to shimmy up the wall of my house to my bedroom window, and he wanted in."

The mourners were stirring uncertainly, apprehensive.

"Of course I was dreaming. You knew I was dreaming, right? There was no way the live Mickey could have shinnied up that wall, he'd have fallen and broken his neck.

"Anyway, I opened the window and Mickey tumbled into the room. We sat on the bed side by side. We talked about a lot of stuff. I don't remember all of it. He complained a lot about the weather, I remember that. We told each other jokes, I remember that, too. He told me one that I didn't get. He always teased, said I was too naïve. He dug his elbow into my ribs so hard, it must have really hurt because it woke me up. I sat up in bed; it was 2:30 in the morning and Mickey was gone.

"Years ago when my dad died, mom assured me that dad would live on because I would always remember him. And she was right. I sometimes see him in a crowd; I hear him laugh; I see him shake his head and hear him say, 'Tsk tsk, Thomas, really,' the way he used to when I did something stupid. That's my point, if there is any point to what I'm saying."

He looked over at the Skruggs children.

He said, "Guys, last night in my mind your Uncle Mickey was still alive, and he'll always be alive because I'll always remember him, and you guys will always remember him, too. Charlie, he'll always be alive because you'll always remember him. All of us will always remember him."

There were nods, a yes or two, an amen from Reverend Paine, followed by others from the rows of mourners. Tommy knew he had said enough. He took his seat beside Callahan, who, misty eyed, took his hand, nodded and lightly touched her lips to his cheek.

CHAPTER 34

There were other speakers, of course, two of whom were of note to Tommy; both were from CCAC.

One was the Assistant Athletic Director, a man of late middle age with gray, brush cut hair and a stiff-jointed stride as if he had blown out both knees. He insisted that the Athletic Department couldn't possibly run smoothly without Michael Skruggs's conscientious efforts. He said it with a straight face, but Tommy hoped it wasn't true, for the school's sake.

The other speaker from CCAC was a co-captain of the Varsity basketball team, who was the only other mourner as tall as the Rev. He added humor to the proceeding—Tommy couldn't tell if it was intentional—when he admitted that he had borrowed $10.00 from Michael and couldn't pay him back because he was still short.

* * *

If you were not acquainted with Michael Skruggs and you were the sort to judge a man by the number of cars in his funeral cortege, you wouldn't think much of Michael as his cortege passed you in the street. But to be fair to those among Mickey's mourners who bailed after the eulogies were concluded, they had been warned by Reverend Paine that the route to the cemetery was long and the interment would be extremely short. So a mere handful of cars followed the hearse and limousine for the interminable trek into the East Hills and beyond to the cemetery.

And true to his word, the Rev's interment ceremony seemed over before it had begun. No sooner had Tommy wondered to himself why the casket was so damned heavy than he was asked to say his final goodbyes. Tommy dumped in a trowel-full of dirt and walked away.

* * *

Callahan and Tommy rode back from the cemetery to Homewood with the family. As they were disembarking the limo in McNeel's parking lot, Marna Skruggs said, "You're following us to the house, aren't you? For a bite to eat and something to drink? Lord knows we could all do with a stiff drink."

Tommy didn't intend to follow them, he intended to drive to their house in Morningside after delivering Callahan to Division 4. He was hungry enough to eat his car's upholstery, and the thought of a stiff drink, preferably a cold beer, made his mouth water.

Callahan said, "Not me, I'm afraid, Marna. I'm on duty this afternoon." She looked at her wristwatch.

"In ten minutes, Tommy. Lieutenant Craig has been on my tail ever since… uh, anyway, all I need is to be late reporting for duty. He'll ream my butt."

That started the kids whispering to each other.

"No, Sash," Charlie Jr. said. "She's a real cop with a gun and everything." Sasha had thought Callahan was a crossing guard.

Sasha didn't know what to do with what her brother just told her, but her eyes were wide and bright with disbelief. She knew not to trust anything he said. She stared at Callahan.

Callahan leaned into the open door of the limo and placed a kiss on Sasha's forehead. Then, without thinking about it, she repeated the lyrics of one of her favorite old songs:

"We are strong, we're invincible, we can do anything. We are woman!"

Charlie and Tommy gaped at each other as the females in the limo fist-bumped.

* * *

After dropping Callahan at Division 4 and promising to be there, as usual, at the end of her shift, Tommy began to weave his way through the maze of narrow, hilly City streets that had to be negotiated in order to attend the wake at the Skruggs house.

Pittsburgh is famously shaped as a triangle formed by, to the north and south, the Allegheny and

Monongahela Rivers, respectively. The two rivers join to point west—Westward Ho!—and become the Ohio. Forming the third side of the triangle, the side without a river or other natural boundary, are the eastern neighborhoods—East Liberty, Morningside, Highland Park, Squirrel Hill, Greenfield, etc. Beyond them are the eastern suburbs. Division 4 is almost dead center in the middle of the eastern base of the triangle, so a crow, even a lazy crow with a wounded wing, could fly from Division 4 in Squirrel Hill to the Skruggs house in Morningside in less than ten minutes. But unless you are a crow, you go nowhere in Pittsburgh in ten minutes at three o'clock on a Friday afternoon—rush hour is already underway. All arteries begin to clog.

But Tommy didn't mind the traffic congestion, he needed to exercise more than the usual caution behind the wheel anyway, since his eyes were blurry with tears. Whenever he thought of his friend Mickey's body in that casket in that hole in the cemetery ground, his eyes would well up. Rarely, he found himself able to focus his mind on Mickey's spirit soaring on its way to heaven, maybe doing loop-the-loops on its way, then Tommy's eyes would clear. When he realized that his stomach was growling with hunger, he leaned more heavily on the gas pedal.

CHAPTER 35

By 6:30 p.m. on Friday evening, the wake for Mickey Skruggs had staggered far beyond a reasonable length, through dusk and into the dark of night. The family and other mourners seemed reluctant to let Mickey's spirit go, as if drinking and overeating had the power to keep him close.

* * *

Meanwhile, Officers Liz Callahan and Joe Lee Gordon were in their vehicle on their way to the Oakland Panera's for a dinner break. Officer Gordon was at the wheel. Their mobile comm unit was constantly squawking—it never stopped squawking—when suddenly this came through:

> *Call for backup. Officer down. Officer down. Qwik-Mart on Boulevard of the Allies. Suspect a lone gunman. Young. Heavily armed and dangerous.*

"The Qwik-Mart on the Boulevard. Jeez, we're close," said Joe Lee.

"I'll respond," Callahan said, reaching for the mic.

Officer Gordon turned the black-and-white left onto the Boulevard, siren whooping, and finally swung into the small parking lot in front of the Qwik-Mart. Broken glass crunched under the vehicle's tires. The store's front windows were blown out. Both officers, weapons in hand, charged to the entrance, Callahan, being the faster of the two, was first in. She almost stumbled over the downed officer, one she didn't know personally but recognized from Oakland's Division 5. He lay on the floor near the door bleeding from a leg wound and yelling into his shoulder mic.

Callahan confronted a young man wearing baggy jeans and a black hoodie. He held some sort of machine pistol loosely in his hand as if it were too heavy for the young man to lift. He was unsteady on his feet, trying unsuccessfully to hold himself erect. Standing seven or eight feet from Callahan, she could see how young he was, how glassy eyed, definitely under the influence of ...something.

The young perp seemed to come awake, to come aware that police officers were confronting him. He found the energy to lift the weapon and point it in their general direction.

Seemingly calm on the outside, anything but calm on the inside, Callahan said, "Drop the weapon. Please drop it, son. Nothing that comes after this is worth your life. Or ours. Please, son, drop it. Now."

He didn't hear her or if he did, he paid no attention. Applied his finger to the trigger and bullets started flying everywhere.

* * *

Tommy emerged from the wake at the Skruggs house into a sharply cold, still and starry night. He filled his chest with a deep draught of air and held it in. It felt to him as if the City, not only he, were holding its breath, anticipating the coming of December, anticipating that something had come to an end and something new was on its way. A deep thought for him. Maybe what he was actually feeling was the alcohol he had consumed.

He drove slowly and cautiously toward Squirrel Hill and Division 4. No way could he pass a Breathalyzer test. He hoped Callahan would be waiting by the door watching for his arrival. That way, he wouldn't have to enter the building fearing he might accidentally breathe on the desk sergeant and get tagged with a DUI. Of course he planned on breathing all over Callahan later that night, but she wouldn't arrest him, would she?

* * *

When Tommy reached Division 4, he found the ambulance bay open but the ambulance gone. Someone was waiting for him in the doorway on the cop side of the building, but it was not Callahan. It was Paul Rafferty, the night shift desk sergeant. He was frantically gesturing for Tommy to park and come inside. Urgently. Tommy eased the Dart into a spot between two black-and-whites and hurried inside.

"Shake a leg!" Rafferty called. He took the stairs to the detective bureau at heart attack speed. He was no spring chicken, Tommy thought, a veteran of fifteen or twenty years. And what did the sergeant say? Something about a shooting? Something about Liz Callahan? Tommy cried out and took the stairs two at a time. He would have passed Rafferty if there had been room.

It seemed to take forever to reach the top of the stairs. The two men stood at the entrance to the detective squad room gasping for breath.

A crowd, some uniformed, some not, circled Detective Goldberg's desk: there was Goldberg, himself, and his partner, Michaels; their boss, Lieutenant Craig; two uniformed officers that Tommy didn't recognize; and Amanda Cummings, civilian staffer. Their constant, buzzing conversation sounded as if someone had poked a stick into a beehive. And surrounded by them, sitting in Goldberg's swivel desk chair, was Callahan, her chin on her chest, looking as if she were half awake, half in a trance. Something made her look up. When she did she saw Tommy and the panic on his face. She leapt to her feet and shouted over the din, "I'm okay, I'm okay!"

She latched onto Tommy's arm, but then she sagged back into the swivel chair and retreated back into herself.

She was definitely not okay—she looked shock-y: cold, pale, her beautiful skin less like malted milk, more like skim. She pulled Tommy close, needing his warmth. She was in no condition to give explanations Tommy turned to her partner, Joe Lee Gordon.

Unlike Callahan, Joe Lee was jazzed. He was bug-eyed, still on his way down from an adrenaline high. His uniform trousers were dusty and his blue shirt was sweat stained.

He said, "We're on our way to get dinner, we're heading to Panera's, y' know, when the call for backup comes in. 'Holdup in progress, the Qwik-Mart, Boulevard of the Allies, suspect armed.' Know the one, Tom? The Quik-Mart on Alllies Boulevard across from the big Greek church? That one, yeah. Well, we're through Schenley Park, on the Boulevard, almost there when, 'Officer Down.' Shit, We're about to pull in. The windows are all blown out, glass everywhere. We run in. There's one cop, a guy from Division 5, laying on the floor, he's yelling and blood is draining from his leg. His partner is ducked down behind the Slurpy machine.

"The guy, this kid really, maybe 18 maybe, I dunno, 20 maybe. He's high as a kite, see, with H or meth or I dunno, and he's got a machine pistol. Don't ask me where he got hold of a fuckin' machine pistol; you can get anything on the street nowadays. You seen one of those, Tom? Looks like a pistol but with a butt and a magazine underneath? Squeeze the trigger once, it keeps on shooting, sprays bullets like a hose. So, anyhoo, this damn druggie starts to spray lead all over the joint, spittin' it out. Bullets flying everywhere, glass exploding, the guy from 5 yelling into his shoulder mic. We're all ducked down behind the Slurpy machine hoping our insurance is paid up, see, and Liz—Wonder Woman here—she asks the guy, real polite-like, 'Please put the gun down, son, please,' and when he doesn't, she puts him down on his ass with one in the chest." Joe Lee's hand became a gun and he popped one at Tommy and blew on his fingers to cool them off. He said, "Fuckin' cool as you please."

Callahan came out of her trance to say, "I wasn't cool, I pissed myself. I had to borrow a pair of Amanda's underpants."

All Tommy could think was, McKenzie was wrong. Thank God, McKenzie was wrong.

The phone rang in Lieutenant Craig's cubbyhole of a private office; he went after it. When he returned, everyone recognized the look on his face though it was a look the Lieutenant rarely showed—indecision. His quandary was: How would Liz Callahan take the latest news?

Lieutenant Craig was Mister Average in every aspect of his appearance. He did have a rather distinctive bulb of a nose and a leprechaun-ish sparkle in his blue eyes. In all other aspects, in height, weight and complexion, he was Mister Average. In intelligence, too. But he was a man of long experience in police work, so this situation was not exactly new to him.

Except this time his officer was a woman.

He stepped back into the squad room and announced without any fanfare, thinking to get it over with as quick as possible, "The perp was DOA on arrival at UPMC Presbyterian."

The noisy room went immediately silent.

* * *

Now Officer Gordon's incident report has been filed and Liz Callahan's official statement has been dictated, printed, signed and endorsed by her partner and one eyewitness from Division 5. A copy has been sent by messenger to UPMC Presbyterian Hospital for the signature of the other eyewitness from Division 5 as soon as he recovers from surgery. The crowd from the detective squad room has dispersed: the detectives left to supervise the processing of the crime scene; the uniformed officers returned to their patrols; the civilian employee walked slowly to her station in records division. Officer Callahan's weapon now resided in Lieutenant Craig's desk drawer, pending formalities to be carried out by the Internal Affairs division and the D.A.'s office.

Callahan and Tommy were now in the Dart still parked in front of the building. They have yet to move, yet to even start the engine. To Callahan it feels as if ice cubes had been held against her flesh until she was totally numb. They sat in the dark and just breathed, finding the dark more comfortable than the fluorescent glare inside the Division house. Callahan was uncharacteristically silent and uncharacteristically still.

"Look," Tommy said, "I don't know what to say to you...except I know where you're at right now. I've just been there. Still am, kind of."

After a moment she said, "I'm sorry if I didn't give you what you needed after you shot Odell Willams. I didn't know what you were going through, not really. I'll try to make up for it, that's a promise."

After a few silent moments she said, "I don't even know his name."

"Who, the perp?"

"The perp. The kid. I don't know his name. They didn't tell me. Maybe they think I don't want to know it. Maybe they think I don't care."

She was going to be angry or she was going to cry, Tommy couldn't tell which. He put his arm around her shoulders and drew her closer to him.

He said, "It's too early for an ID unless he was carrying a wallet in his pocket. They know you, Hon. All those guys do. They know you care."

Callahan said, "They're a little pumped right now. Especially Joe Lee."

"A little, yeah."

"What a couple we are, huh, Tommy. Murdoch and Callahan, Wyatt Earp and Doc Holliday. Gunfighters at the OK Corral."

He said, "The Squirrel Hill Corral."

"Very funny, very goddamn funny."

He held her while she wept.

CHAPTER 36

They had been alternating between sleeping at her place and his, so in the early hours of Saturday, before there were any signs of dawn, they staggered up to Tommy's carriage house apartment. Bobbi leapt out of her crate at the sound of their feet on the stairs. Bobbi almost never barked—growled deep in her throat, yes, but barked, almost never. The so called beagle's bark, more a croak than a bark, seemed to embarrass her. This time, however, she barked, demanding hugs and kisses from both of them.

Bobbi's enthusiasm was almost too much to bear. The day that was now finally behind them—and what a day it had been, with the funeral, the wake and the shooting at the Quik-Mart—Friday had totally emotionally drained them. As soon as they managed to get Bobbi calmed down, they struggled out of their clothes and fell into Tommy's bed in their underwear. By the time Tommy managed to unhook her bra, Callahan had fallen asleep.

* * *

There was not much left of the day when they finally re-surfaced on Saturday afternoon. They could tell by peeking out at the courtyard beneath the bedroom window that the sunlight—or what little there had been of it in the first place—would be gone in no more than an hour.

Bobbi had emptied her bowl of kibble, late as it had come, and literally polished the empty bowl with her tongue. Now she was out on a lead behind the carriage house taking care of business.

The couple sat at the dinette table in Tommy's tiny kitchen. Callahan was wrapped in Tommy's heavy winter robe. They wore glossy-eyed dazes on their faces, from too little sleep or too much, one or the other, and as the aftermath of the previous day's events. Over orange juice in jelly glasses and stale-but-edible-if-toasted English muffins, they tried to plan what remained of the weekend.

She was on leave until the Internal Affairs Department released its report justifying or not justifying the shooting—a mere formality in this case, they both knew, there being so many eyewitnesses.

She said, "Whatever else we do tomorrow, I need to go to church. I haven't been to church since my father died." It appeared to stun her when she realized it had been three years. "It doesn't matter which church we go to. Any one will do. How about where you said you go sometimes, Temple Israel? That'll do, your rabbi can hear my confession."

The last thing Tommy wanted to do was embarrass her, so he stifled his laugh.

He said, "Wrong on two counts. Temple Israel doesn't have services on Sundays; Friday nights and Saturday mornings, yes, but not Sundays. On Sundays you use crayons to color pictures of the Hebrews crossing the Red Sea."

He realized he'd thrown her a curve ball.

He said, "I'm talking about Sunday School. That's all I remember ever doing in Sunday School, coloring pictures with crayons. And besides, rabbis aren't priests, they don't hear confessions."

Callahan said, "I told you I had a lot to learn."

She gave it another minute's thought while she drank some of her orange juice.

She said, "How about Reverend Paine's church… the something of the Redeemer? I like him, don't you?"

"It's the First Church of the Redeemer." Tommy certainly did like Reverend Paine. He said he wouldn't mind at all attending one of the Rev's services, but he remembered the Rev saying that he was a Baptist minister, not a Catholic, and that he didn't hear confessions.

She replied, "Hearing confessions must be a nasty job, so few want to do it."

"I guess. Besides," he said, reaching across the table to rest a hand on hers, "I bet most people who need to confess, don't, and those who don't need to confess, do. You, for instance. I don't see that you have anything to confess. No more than I did, surely. You did what you had to do under the circumstances, didn't you? Just like I did? Isn't that what you told me? So, what could a priest say that would make any difference?"

"I haven't a clue what a priest would say or how it would help. But I have to try, Tommy. I won't feel right unless I try."

"I understand."

More than anyone else could understand or feel, Tommy thought he understood and felt her distress. Before this moment he thought he had already climbed that fence and thought he was on the other side of it. Now he had reason to doubt that. Could he give her a hand over the fence? He'd try with jokes.

He said, "Occasionally my Dad used to take me to Saint Paul's Cathedral in Oakland, especially around Christmastime. What a grand place, but overwhelming for a child. I remember the first time I saw people going in and out of those little booths. I asked Dad to loan me a dime so I could make a phone call."

A valiant effort on Tommy's part, but it didn't look as if it had worked. He thought it was worth another try.

He said, "I never took Communion; Mom would've hit the ceiling, but I did confess a few times." His voice slid into a childlike falsetto. " 'Bless me, Father, for I have sinned.' But, I admit, when I confessed I fibbed a lot, and I never confessed when I did anything bad."

"I can't imagine you ever doing anything bad, Tommy. Besides, kids aren't sinners, they're not really responsible."

"Well, maybe I wasn't fibbing. Maybe I was just withholding evidence." Like I did at the hearing, he thought, withholding that I goaded Odell Willams. "But you're right," he said, "kids aren't responsible, only adults are."

He realized he was hardly in a position to help her over the fence, he still needed a hand, himself.

"Okay," he said. "Saint Paul's it is, tomorrow morning. I agree, it's worth a try."

Chapter 37

Tommy awoke early on Sunday morning to the sound of rain drumming on the roof and lightly tapping on the bedroom window. It seemed to be in sync with the regular beat of Callahan's heart. She had fallen asleep with the weight of her body against his side, her head on his shoulder, her hair in his ear, on his cheek.

The monotone of the rain had put him in a wistful mood. He felt the rain was a Godsend, tapping out a message to him, blessing his coupling with Callahan. He was glad they planned to attend Saint Paul's that morning, grateful for the opportunity to thank Him for the blessing. Still, he found it odd to think of God as Him; whenever he thought of God, he pictured a darkly serene, eastern European beauty—his mother.

Two rain-drenched cars sat in the courtyard below: his Dart that they had abandoned in front of the carriage house; and a black sedan Tommy recognized as the Mercury Milan that belonged to Arthur's executive assistant, Marge Tangretti. The Merc was parked close to the rear of the main house. Now what was Marge doing there on a Sunday morning?

Callahan joined him at the window. She clung to him, shivering, and sought his warmth. She yawned and said, "Time zit?"

"Nearly seven."

"Come back to bed."

Yes. He did.

* * *

Two hours later when next they returned to look out the bedroom window, they saw the rain had given over to flurries and the bullying wind was kicking dead leaves into the air. The night had been mild, but here was evidence that December was about to happen. They turned away from the window and went to shower and dress, then headed down to the car. Tommy held her door and was about to help her in when...

"Hey! Hold up, Lunkhead!" Arthur yelled from his position at the kitchen door. When he saw that his brother wasn't alone, he called, "Hey, wait up, you guys." He hurried to the car, and when he got there he went straight to Callahan.

He had received a full report from Police Headquarters as to what went down at the Qwik-Mart, heard tales of Elizabeth Callahan's bravery, heard that an award ceremony was being planned by the police brass. When he mentioned a commendation and a medal, Callahan was aghast.

She held Arthur by both hands and begged, "Can you do anything, anything at all, to put the kibosh to those plans? Please, Arthur. You're the D.A. Surely you have clout with the Police Department. Please, Arthur, for me?"

"But, why? Why not take the accolades you deserve?"

He found his answer swimming around in deep pools of anxiety and regret at having taken a life in Elizabeth's eyes. The same anxiety and regret he had seen before and could still see in his brother's eyes.

He said, "Forget I asked, okay? If you're serious about stopping it, I'll see what I can do."

Callahan placed a kiss on his cheek and thanked him.

"I'll try to get it done with a phone call or two before we leave for Philadelphia."

Tommy had been wondering why Arthur was dressed so nice, not his usual Sunday morning schlumpies, as their mother used to say, but one of his gray pinstripe suits. And he was wondering why Marge was there.

Artie said, "I'm off to attend a conference of the PAADA in Philly. A big deal of an annual event."

Tommy said, "Why would you attend a meeting of the Dental Society?"

Arthur rolled his eyes. "The Pennsylvania Association of District Attorneys, you dipstick. Three days of boredom and bullshit, but it's on the County, all expenses paid."

Callahan said, "I'll bet the wives love shopping in downtown Philadelphia."

"You can say that again. Nina will shop till she drops. Marge is staying with the girls."

Tommy said, "Aha. I recognized her car."

Artie looked at Callahan, nodded at Tommy.

He said, "Quite a detective, my little brother."

Then he said, "Speaking of shopping, Elizabeth," Arthur said, "About a certain ring in a certain safe deposit box. Nina says it will be perfect for you, and I agree. So. Marge has the address and phone number of the jeweler we recommend. They're on the fourth floor of the Clark Building downtown. Know where I mean?"

She did. She said, "You mean, in the wholesale district."

"That's the place. Give them a call and ask for Mrs. Katz."

"Mrs. Katz. Got it."

"She's a genius with mountings. One look at you and one look at the stone in Mom's ring, she'll know just how to mount it so it'll look great on your left hand." He nodded toward Tommy again as he spoke to Callahan. "Make sure he calls, makes an appointment. Or else you do it."

Then Arthur turned away toward the house.

"Oh, and there's this." He reached into a pocket of his suit coat and came up with a tiny red envelope. "In case…"

Tommy chimed in, nastily mimicking Arthur, "In case my lunkhead of a little brother lost his key to the safe deposit box." Then in his normal voice, "For your info, Artie, I didn't lose my key, and…"

Callahan interrupted, "But it was sweet of him to think of it, wasn't it, Tommy?"

She looked from one brother to the other, knowing that her destiny was to be a peacemaker between the brothers. Maybe she and Nina working together…

She said, "Boy, do I wish I had a big brother to look after me."

"You do," Tommy said, aiming his thumb at Arthur. "Him."

There was a moment of tension that threatened to flare up like a fourth of July rocket, but instead it fizzled into laughter and a three-way hug.

The end